F
GRA

Grant, Bruce

PANCHO

PANCHO

A Dog of the Plains

PANCHO

A Dog of the Plains

by Bruce Grant

Illustrated by PAUL GALDONE

THE WORLD PUBLISHING COMPANY

CLEVELAND AND NEW YORK

Published by The World Publishing Company
2231 West 110th Street, Cleveland 2, Ohio

Published simultaneously in Canada by
Nelson, Foster & Scott Ltd.

Library of Congress Catalog Card Number: 58-9417

FIRST EDITION

FIDELITY

The story of the faithfulness of the dog Pancho is a true one. For almost two weeks he remained alone on guard in a lonely section of southwest Texas, after he had been instructed by his masters to stay there. Sergeant James B. Gillett, one of the party who rescued Pancho, later wrote in his book *Six Years With the Texas Rangers*: "The Rangers were as much delighted as if it had been a human being they had rescued. . . . That Mexican shepherd dog is entitled to a monument on which should be inscribed 'Fidelity.' " And so on this page is inscribed the word "Fidelity" for Pancho and all other faithful dogs, and the book itself is dedicated to Lea and Blair Wolfram and all other girls and boys who love and appreciate their pets.

Contents

PANCHO

A Dog of the Plains

1. Pancho Finds an Enemy and a Friend

PANCHO CAME to a stop at the top of the hill. He raised his head and sniffed. Below him was a narrow, winding stream of water hardly wider than a creek. A dog of Pancho's size could easily walk across it without wetting the hair on his back.

To Pancho this stream was merely a slowly moving body of water. It meant nothing to him that on the American side it was called the Rio Grande, the grand or great river, and on the Mexican side the Río Bravo del Norte, the brave or savage river of the north. Nor could he reason

11

that although it was very low now, at times it was wild and fierce and overflowed its banks and swept everything before it.

Pancho stood and sniffed, and his eyes searched the country across the river. It was not what he saw—the rolling ground with scattered trees and patches of yellow earth or the tall mountains rising in the background—that interested him, but what he smelled. The slight breeze from across the river brought to Pancho some long-forgotten scent. It brought to him a smell vaguely familiar, one that he tried hard to place.

The breeze was gentle and warm and certainly a relief from the cold January wind which had been blowing from the north earlier that day. But that smell? Pancho sniffed and sniffed and whined a little. Perhaps the smell came from the pueblo, a small cluster of adobe houses, just at the foot of the hill on this side of the river. No, it was the smell not just of a pueblo, but of a land, of a country. The fact that Mexico, the place of his birth, was just across that river could not be known to Pancho; but somehow he sensed it from the smell that came from those plains.

Pancho was a large dog, black all over with short glossy hair. Only a streak of white showed on his right side where an old wound had healed.

His face was long and narrow, his head broad between his brown eyes. Unlike most shepherd dogs, who are trained not to bite and whose lower jaws are slender, Pancho's underjaw was heavy and strong, much like a wolf's. His ears were pointed, and when he became excited at some sound they pricked at the ends.

He stood now, his mouth open in a grin, his long red tongue hanging from his jowls, his ears pricked, his bushy tail waving back and forth. His black nostrils fluttered as he sniffed, and his breath came out in a puzzled whimper. Then his ears flicked back. The horses were coming up the hill behind him.

They all had traveled a long distance that day. They had been a long time on the way—all the way from the Arizona silver-mine fields. Fields where men found shiny white metal which seemed to interest them more than hunting, chasing wild mustangs, herding cattle, or any of the other things that interest dogs. Yes, in the latter part of the 1870's men flocked to that territory, braving the heat of the desert, the terror of the bloodthirsty Apaches, the lack of food, to pick up that shiny metal. "Balls of silver as big as your fist . . ." some reported.

But Pancho had enjoyed the trip. He liked going

places. He always trotted in the lead, making side tours now and then to pick up a scent, to chase a cottontail or a roadrunner, to investigate here and there—always alert for the smell of an Apache. Pancho hated Apaches. There was nothing he hated as much as Apaches.

Always behind Pancho during the march came the two horses hitched to a covered, swaying vehicle called an "ambulance." These ambulances, which had once been used during wartime, were convenient and comfortable. They looked much like stagecoaches, but were canvas-covered. Bill Wiswald sat on the driver's seat, letting the horses follow Pancho, who had been started in the right direction that morning. Behind the ambulance rode Jack Andrews on his saddle pony. Sometimes he rode alongside the ambulance, and other times he rode up with Pancho. Occasionally Jack changed off with Bill, who got on the pony while Jack drove the team. It had been that way for days.

Now the two horses neared the top of the hill. As they approached, Pancho did not move from their path. He merely flicked his ears back when Bill shouted, "There it is—the Rio Grande!"

Jack rode his pony ahead and pulled up beside Pancho. "Yes, that's it all right," he said.

Just then Pancho growled. His forefeet spread and he braced himself more firmly. His nose lowered and pointed down. The hair on his neck began to rise in an angry furrow, and then it stood up along his back. His tail bristled.

"What's the matter, Pancho?" asked Jack. "What's wrong, boy?" He turned and called to Bill, "Pancho sees something he doesn't like."

From the rise on which they had halted, the two men could survey the country before them. Directly below was a pueblo of adobe houses. Coming toward them from the pueblo was a man on horseback, leading two other horses. Pancho was looking directly at this group. He continued to growl. "What's the matter with that dog?" asked Jack, flicking his quirt.

"I wouldn't do that," warned Bill, who thought Jack was going to strike Pancho. "From the way he looks that would set him off. He might start out after those horses and that man. Take it easy, Jack." He spoke soothingly to the dog. "What's the matter, boy? What's wrong?"

The man and horses turned off to the left. The man was taking them to the clump of trees just under the hill, perhaps to a spring of fresh water.

Pancho watched them go until they disappeared

among the trees. Gradually the hair flattened on his back and neck; his head went up and again he sniffed the air. Then, as if for the first time realizing the two men were beside him, he turned and wagged his tail. He reared up and placed his paws on the shoulders of Jack's horse, and Jack leaned over and scratched his ear. Pancho dropped to all fours and went to the side of the ambulance and placed his paws on the wheel nearest Bill, who patted him.

"Something about that man or those horses bothered him," said Jack.

"Yes, something," replied Bill. He let the reins fall flat on the backs of the horses. "Get up!" he said.

"That can't be El Paso, but maybe we'll get some information there," said Jack. He leaned forward in his saddle and loosened the reins. His pony started downhill.

Pancho ran ahead, darting back and forth, giving short, happy barks. Once or twice he stopped, turned his head toward the clump of trees, and lifted his nose.

"Still not satisfied," laughed Bill above the screech of the wheel brake as the ambulance began to roll down the hill.

They followed a rough dirt road. It was the middle of the afternoon, and the sun beat down. The faint breeze from across the river could not be felt in the valley.

Then the dog and saddle pony and ambulance came into a narrow street. There was no one in the street; it was like a city of the dead. But the two men knew it was the siesta hour—that time in the afternoon when everyone rested.

Pancho went ahead warily, sniffing here and there. He wanted to be sure there was no danger. Jack rode ahead of the team of horses. "Look at all these doors and window sills painted blue," he said.

"Indians believe that keeps the devils out," laughed Bill. "This is an Indian pueblo."

The little procession, led by Pancho, came into the pueblo plaza. There still was no one in sight. Even though it was winter, the weather was warm and the sun bright and hot. Everyone was inside in the shade, resting or sleeping.

But soon they were greeted by a shout: "Look! There comes a big black bear!"

"That's not a bear—that's a big black wolf."

"Get your guns, boys. There's a man-eating mountain lion."

"Mountain lions don't have tails, not bob-tailed mountain lions."

Pancho, who had entered the plaza first, hesitated, one forefoot raised and his head lowered, like a pointer. But he did not growl.

Bill drew on the reins and brought the horses to a halt. "Hello!" he called.

From the shade of an adobe hut several men who had been sitting, or lying down, got up. One of them stretched his arms over his head and yawned.

"Welcome, strangers," called another. He started to advance toward them, but on seeing Pancho, he changed his mind and remained where he was.

"Don't worry about him," laughed Jack. "Pancho won't hurt you."

Jack got down from his pony and went to the dog's side, placing his hand on Pancho's neck. Pancho turned his head and wagged his tail.

But he watched the other men out of the corner of his eye. He was not sure. He began to sniff the air. He could detect no unfriendly smell.

"Better watch him; he was acting funny back there," said Bill.

Jack patted Pancho's neck again and then walked ahead, his hand extended. "My name's Andrews—Jack Andrews," he said.

"I'm Jim Gault, Texas Rangers, Frontier Battalion."

"Texas Rangers!" exclaimed Jack. "What are Texas Rangers doing here in this place?"

"Injuns—Apaches," said Jim Gault, briefly. He evidently thought that was enough to say about that subject.

"That's my partner," said Jack, waving toward Bill.

Pancho did not move. Jim Gault glanced quickly at him, circled around him muttering something about "big dog," and went to the side of the wagon, where he shook hands with Bill.

"Nice outfit you've got here," Jim commented. "Settlers?"

"No, we're miners," said Bill. "We're from Colorado—been in Arizona. Now on our way to San Antonio."

"Well, make yourselves at home here; there's plenty of room," said Jim. "Lieutenant Baylor's over in Mexico with most of the men, chasing that renegade, Victorio. He's broken loose again."

"Victorio?" questioned Jack Andrews.

"Sure, Victorio, the Apache—he's on the warpath again."

Pancho gave a low growl, and Jim Gault stepped back. "Acts like he understands," he said, grinning.

"Maybe he doesn't like Apaches very much either."

"He's got a right not to, I guess," said Jack, laying his hand on Pancho's neck. "But I think we'll accept your hospitality. We've had a long trip." He looked around him. "What town is this? We expected to reach El Paso today."

"Oh, this is Ysleta—ees-lay-tah," Jim pronounced it carefully. "Old Tiwa Indian pueblo—friendly Indians, they are. Some just call them Pueblo Indians. El Paso's just a few miles up the river there."

Several other Rangers had joined them, making a big circle around Pancho, who eyed them indifferently.

"Never seen a bigger dog if that's what he is," said one.

"Almost as big as a burro."

"But heavier, I'll bet."

Pancho sank on his haunches, his mouth open and tongue thrust forward, his ears moving backward and forward, picking up every sound. Jack kept his hand on Pancho's neck, and now and then Pancho twisted his head and licked his master's hand.

While the Rangers and miners were talking, a small boy came up noiselessly. Pancho saw him and rose on all fours. Jack felt the dog move and looked down at him and then at the boy. He caught the loose skin of Pancho's neck with both hands.

"Keep that boy away!" he cried. "He's an Indian, and Pancho doesn't like Indians."

"That's Little Jim," said Jim Gault. "Named for me. He's a good boy, a Pueblo Indian. He won't hurt anyone . . . his pa and ma were killed by Apaches——"

"Tell him not to come close to this dog!"

But if Little Jim heard, he paid no attention. He came on, his moccasins making no sound. He walked directly toward Pancho.

Pancho pulled hard to get to the boy, and Jack held tighter. "I'm warning you, I won't be responsible!" he shouted.

"That dog's waggin' his tail. He wants to play," said Jim Gault, making no attempt to stop Little Jim.

Little Jim walked right up to Pancho, who was straining his neck. Jack sought to step between Pancho and Little Jim, but Pancho pulled to the side. Little Jim reached out and placed a hand on Pancho's head, and rubbed the dog's ears. Pancho gave a series of whines. He smelled the boy all over—his moccasins, his half-naked, nut-brown body. Pancho's nose moved over the boy's

face, and then out came his tongue and he licked him.

Little Jim talked all the while in low, singsong Mexican. He called Pancho *perrito,* which means "little dog."

Jack looked at Pancho and Little Jim as if he could not believe what he saw. He could not understand Pancho allowing a stranger—an Indian at that—to pet him; nor could he believe anyone could be so brave as to walk up in this manner to such a big, fierce-looking dog as Pancho.

"I can't believe my eyes," he said with a shrug.

"Well, Injuns and animals can tell right off whether a man or another animal is friendly," chuckled Jim Gault. "You can't fool 'em. They're both sons of nature, and they have their ways of knowin' things you and me can't understand."

"Guess so," replied Jack, letting go of Pancho's neck. Pancho just stood, eyes half closed, while Little Jim rested an arm on his back. Little Jim did not have to bend over to rest his arm on Pancho.

"You just bring your wagon over to that last adobe house on the right of the plaza," said Jim Gault. "Lieutenant Baylor should be back in a day or so if you care to wait. You better talk to him before you start on your way. These Apaches sure are bloodthirsty——"

Pancho gave a low growl. He wheeled around, almost knocking down Little Jim. Jim Gault was about to comment on how well Pancho understood the name "Apache." But then they saw what was exciting Pancho.

The horseman they had seen previously from the top of the hill was riding toward them. There was no doubt now that Pancho had taken a dislike to this man. He bared his teeth, gave a warning growl, and prepared to leap toward the man when Jack's sharp command came. "Down, Pancho!"

Pancho obeyed instantly. He crouched at Jack's feet, but continued to growl.

"That's Jack One Day," announced Jim Gault. "Your dog doesn't seem to cotton to him. He's one of our Apache scouts."

"Apache!" exclaimed Jack. He reached down and rubbed Pancho's head. "Apache . . . well, that explains it."

2. Why Pancho Hated Apaches

PANCHO LAY on his belly in the doorway of the adobe hut. His head rested on one outstretched foreleg, but every so often he raised it slightly and looked out into the plaza. He sniffed the night air. Some sounds brought forth a low throaty growl, which faded away as his head fell back on his foreleg.

It was his duty to watch throughout the night and Pancho rarely slept. When he did sleep, it was a very light sleep, and he was usually restless. His sleep seemed troubled and the skin on his back twitched as if to throw off something. He would whine like a puppy.

25

Suddenly he would awaken fully and then he would be very still, his muscles tense and his great body prepared for instant action. He would look warily about him and breathe in all the odors of night. If none disturbed him, he would sigh and begin to lick the streak of white hair on his right side, where long ago a nasty wound had healed. There was no need for him to lick that spot, for the place no longer hurt him. It was a habit he had when anything disturbed him. It had been a bad wound which had taken a long time to heal.

His masters always knew when Pancho had been excited about something. "Now, watch him, he'll lick that white streak on his side," Jack would say.

"Yes, there he goes," Bill would reply. "That place certainly doesn't bother him after all these years. He must have had a bad cut or something when he was a puppy. I've felt all around that spot, and it doesn't hurt him. I can't figure it out."

Jack and Bill would very much have liked to know just what went on in Pancho's mind at such times. Pancho's action amused them, just as they were amused when he was playful and started chasing his own tail, whirling around and around in a frantic fashion. Or when he would suddenly dash away at top speed and return carrying a stick in his mouth, which he would place at the feet of one of them. Then he would brace himself for another dash, showing that he wanted them to throw it so he could bring it back.

What causes dogs to chase their tails? Is it a flea or a tick that bothers them? Apparently it isn't anything of the sort, for they do it in fun. They seem to enjoy it, and do it as naturally as they scratch when tickled on a certain rib or their "funny bone." And what about chasing and bringing back a stick or rock? It is a game, nothing more. All dogs do this and seem to relish the sport.

And why did Pancho, after a disturbing dream of some sort, and even after lying in the shade, his eyes half-closed as if thinking of things of long ago, suddenly begin to lick that long-healed wound? Just a matter of habit, one might say.

Whatever went on in that dream or in those thoughts brought Pancho's mind back to the time he got that cut, or slash. That had been long ago in Pancho's life. He was now perhaps five or six years old, the equivalent in a dog's life of about thirty-five years of a man's life. He had then been a puppy of perhaps eight months by man-made reckoning. Pancho wouldn't remember where he was then, but should he ever return there now, he would certainly know. There would be certain things which would recall the place to mind. He would have some sort of feeling he was back on familiar ground. Perhaps a smell of some kind. Maybe just instinct.

He had been one of seven puppies—all awkward, big-footed, black with longer ears than usual, cold, damp noses, healthy appetites, and much curiosity. His large black-haired mother was just a dining room where the best puppy-food was to be had, a nice warm belly where the best sleep could be had, a cleaning establishment where burrs and dirt and matted hair were taken care of by strong teeth and a long, rough tongue. She maintained a place of refuge in time of danger and a school where dog-manners were taught with sharp teeth and a hefty paw. Pancho's brothers and sisters were creatures with whom to tussle, chase and bite playfully, and curl up with next to their mother.

Pancho would neither recall them in his thinking moments, nor in his dreams. That was not a dog's way. However, he would have recognized them if he ever ran across them again; but this would never be. Nor would he recall his father, much larger than his mother, much stronger—a giant as dogs went, with wolflike jaws, iron muscles, a stern and forbidding manner. When his father, a Mexican shepherd dog, returned from a day's hard work tending a herd of irritating and exasperating sheep, and even long-horned cattle, he did not wish to be bothered. If Pancho or any other of the puppies went near him, he growled a warning that could not be misunderstood. Dignified and serious, he was their lord and master. Perhaps Pancho hoped someday to be like him. Certainly now he was as huge and as iron-muscled and as proud.

No, Pancho would neither have remembered the rancho in Chihuahua—the great cattle-and-sheep ranch which nestled beneath the Candelaria Mountains—nor the ranchero, Don José Osornio, a proud and handsome man who traced his ancestry back to the conquistadors. He wouldn't have remembered the day Don José looked into the hayrack and saw Pancho's mother resting on her side, with a squirming mass of black-haired puppies, their eyes as yet unopened, pushing and nuzzling for their food.

Don José had poked into the wriggling mass with his *cuarta*, or short-handled quirt, and said,

"That one—that big one, see? He will be like his father."

If Pancho ever met Don José again, his instinct would recall the man to him. But that, too, would never be. One night during the full moon—the Apache Moon, for the Apaches struck at night only when there was light—there had been piercing war cries, screams, curses, noise of gunfire, crackling of flames, shouts of horsemen, and squealing of horses. The Apaches had come! Pancho's father had met them at the barn, and with angry growls, flashing teeth, and foam-flecked mouth had torn one rider from his horse. He just reared up and dragged him from the saddle, shaking him as little Pancho might have shaken a field mouse. He went on shaking him, even though a lance hurled by another Indian pierced him through and through. Then there was a fiendish slaughter of every creature in sight. Knives, lances, tomahawks, and finally fire.

It was in this slaughter that Pancho received the long cut in his side. He had crawled away, whimpering at first, but then quieting down when he found refuge beneath a pile of logs. That was the first time, too, that his keen puppy's nose scented these strange, fierce men. It was a smell he would never forget, a smell he would always associate with danger. He did not recall any of this, of course, for dogs do not think in this way. But a smell brought back a warning, even a smell in a kind of dream, as it were. It was then that Pancho licked the long-healed wound that had left a streak of white on his night-black body.

After supper the men sat in the adobe house where the Rangers lived. Jim Gault and the other Rangers wanted to know about Pancho. Jim said he guessed Pancho was the finest-looking dog he had ever seen, and asked Jack how he and Bill had gotten him. As Jack answered he let his hand rest on Pancho's head. The dog sat beside him. Beside Pancho was Little Jim.

"Bill and I were looking for silver in Arizona," he said, nodding toward his partner. "You remember there were stories about balls of silver being found in that territory. All you had to do was to walk along and pick them up. People soon found out different. So we went in to find our silver by hard work.

"Anyway, a Mexican came into our camp one evening, and he had this dog. The Mexican was down on his luck, and he wanted to sell us two burros he had. We didn't need his burros, but we offered to buy the dog. He said he wouldn't sell Pancho; he said there wasn't another one like him in all Mexico.

"The more he refused to sell, the more anxious Bill and I were to have Pancho. Especially after the Mexican showed us a few of the things Pancho could do. For instance, he said, he never had to stake out or hobble his horses and burros at night. All he had to do was to tell Pancho to watch them, and he could be certain they would be there in the morning.

"He got up and took the packs from his two burros and let them go. They didn't need any urging. Apparently they wanted to go back to Mexico, so they started south. The Mexican came back, rolled a cigarette, and calmly smoked it. After an hour or so he leaned over and said to Pancho, 'Go and get them, *amigo*.' The dog bounded up and started in the direction the two burros had taken. The Mexican spread out his blankets and went to bed.

"But Bill and I were too curious to see what the dog did, so we sat up and waited. In a couple of hours we heard a noise, and a few minutes later the two burros showed up, with Pancho herding them. Then he stood guard over them the rest of the night. When the Mexican awoke in the morning his burros were there, as he knew they would be. He certainly hadn't worried about Pancho not bringing them back."

"Yes, and after that we were determined to have this dog," added Bill. "I was pretty sure the Mexican had put the dog through his paces just so he could get more money for him. Jack felt that way, too. We counted out one hundred silver dollars and laid them in front of the Mexican at breakfast. He shrugged and picked up the money. Then he called Pancho to him, put his arm around his neck, and lifted one ear and whispered something into it."

Jack picked up the story. "As the Mexican talked we could see the dog turn toward us, looking first at one and then at the other. You won't believe it, but I'm sure Pancho nodded his head. We asked the man what he had said to Pancho. He replied that he had explained to him that he was a poor man and had to sell him, and that Pancho must remain with his new masters and mind them as he had minded him."

"Now, wait a little minute," interrupted Jim Gault. "I'm listening carefully to all this, and I guess the other boys are too. There's not a man jack of us hasn't been around animals all his life.

Some of us believe that animals, especially hosses, can think, and some are of the opinion they can't. I believe they can think to a certain extent. I believe too——"

"What about some of those old mossy horns that live in the chaparral," cut in Long Pete, another Ranger. "If those critters can't think of more devilment in a split second than any blood-thirsty Apaches——"

"Whoa, now," said Jim Gault. "Let me say what I'm trying to say. I believe animals can think, but I'm not going so far as to swallow all this about Pancho listening and nodding his head when his master was talking to him."

"I just said I thought he nodded his head," laughed Jack. "Perhaps I was mistaken. It doesn't matter about that, but the Mexican left the dog behind—just rode away without looking back—and Pancho did as his owner had said. He stayed right with us, and he has minded us at all times."

Jim Gault lifted his huge shoulders and threw out his hands, palms up. "I'm not one to dispute what you say, mister," he replied. "I guess you know what you're talking about. But what I want to know is where did this Mexican get such a dog, and him saying there wasn't another one like him in all Mexico?"

"I forgot," said Jack. "He did explain that. He said about three years before he and some others, who had banded together after the Apaches had come down from New Mexico, raiding and killing, had arrived at the ranch of a wealthy man named—well, I've forgotten his name. They found the ranch in ruins, everyone killed, the cattle and sheep scattered, and all the horses gone. He found this dog with a deep gash in his side, whimpering under a pile of logs. He put the little fellow in his saddlebag and carried him away, and later treated his wound and made him well."

Jim Gault scratched the stubble on his chin. "Now let me think," he said. "That must have been the time that Geronimo and some of the younger Apache chiefs went on the warpath when the Government wanted to move them from Arizona. Geronimo went down into Sonora mainly, but some of his men went over into Chihuahua, raiding and killing like always."

"Guess maybe you are right," said Jack. "But what's all the Indian trouble now? You see, we came down from the north."

"It's old Victorio, like I told you," said Jim Gault. "But the same trouble. These Injuns don't like reservations."

3. The Two Friends

Pancho and Little Jim walked together across the pueblo plaza, the boy's hand resting on Pancho's back. Pancho walked along proudly, turning his head now and then toward Little Jim and looking sideways at him. Pancho held his tail high and gave it a side-to-side wag.

Little Jim talked softly to Pancho in Mexican, and Pancho seemed to answer now and then with an understanding whimper. "Do you see my friend, Don Jaime Gault, and your master, Don Juan Andrews, talking over there, my friend? They are talking about us. I can tell by the way they look

at us. They see we are great friends, and they are
happy for us. Is it not the truth?"

Pancho thought it was. He expressed himself
with a whimper.

"Now, Don Francisco," continued Little Jim. "I
call you Don Francisco, for the name Pancho is
not one for a fine gentleman-dog such as you.
Pancho is the short way to say Francisco, and I
shall call you Don Francisco, and you must call
me Don Jaime. Is that not right?"

"Yes," agreed Pancho, or Don Francisco, with
his whimper.

"Now we will take a walk to the edge of town.
We will be on the lookout for *el capitán*, who is
to return this afternoon. You come with me?"

"Of course," agreed Pancho.

"We will leave those two to discuss us in their
way. Let us go."

Little Jim began to run. Pancho first looked
toward Jack Andrews as if asking permission, and
seeing Jack wave his hand, he bounded after the
boy, running in circles around him and barking
gaily.

Jim Gault and Jack Andrews were in fact dis-
cussing Little Jim and Pancho. "Looks like you

done lost that dog of yours," Jim said, as he paused in cleaning his carbine in the shade of the adobe. He pointed with his ramrod toward Pancho and Little Jim.

Jack Andrews laughed. "They certainly seem to take to each other," he said.

Jim Gault looked around carefully as if he wished not to be overheard, and leaned toward Jack. "I didn't want to say anything about it, mister," he began in a low voice, "but it's plumb natural for this boy and dog to like each other right off. When you told about that Mexican feller explaining to you how he had picked up this pup after an Apache raid, you might have been telling the story of Little Jim there."

"You mean?" asked Jack.

"Yes, that's what I mean. It was in a pueblo to the north of here. We came in just after the Apaches had attacked the place. They sure did a good job. I guess they didn't kill too many of the Pueblo Indians, but they sure did run them off somewhere. They wrecked the village and took all the horses. Well, I come across this boy half-buried under an adobe wall that had been knocked down. They had got his parents, and I guess everyone kin to him. He was a brave little lad, and he wasn't crying or even whimpering. Right then and there, I reckon, he was figuring out how he would some day get even with them Apaches."

"And so you brought him back here?"

"Yep, I took him up behind me on the hoss and brought him here," said Jim Gault. "Now, he's a smart little fellow. He speaks Injun and Mexican, of course. And you wouldn't believe it, but he speaks American better than me. Seems he had already been going to some church school."

"How long ago was it that you found him?"

"Oh, that was back last summer when we first come out here." Jim Gault paused and rubbed his carbine barrel with his hand. "He had some Injun name, but they got to calling him Little Jim after me, see? So we call him Little Jim."

Jack said nothing. He was thinking. Finally he spoke. "Jim, why don't you let us take that boy to San Antonio? I know my partner, Bill, would approve. We can put Little Jim in a school there. We won't be taking him away from you. You can see him when you get back there. He should have a chance at an education."

Jim Gault got up, shuffled his feet, and for a moment looked unhappy. Then his tanned, seamed face brightened into a smile. "I reckon you are right, mister," he said. "This lad should have a chance. But there would be certain things to talk over with the Government. You just can't take an Injun boy away like that"—he snapped his fingers—"you'd have to explain things."

"I don't believe there would be much difficulty about that," said Jack.

Jim Gault looked pleased, and then he frowned. Afterward he seemed pleased again, but in a different way. "Maybe that boy wouldn't want to leave—to leave—us Rangers," he said hopefully. "You couldn't take him unless he wanted to go."

Jack Andrews understood. Jim Gault did not want to part with Little Jim. "He wouldn't forget you," said Jack. "We'd see to that. And, like I said, you would see him when you returned to San Antonio."

"Well, I reckon maybe it would be all right; it would be the best for him," Jim said finally. "We'll talk to him."

Pancho and Little Jim reached the river bank. A steep place showed the water level when the river was its usual size. But the river was low now, and the bottom of hard, cracked mud sloped down on both sides.

"Come on, Don Francisco," called Little Jim,

letting himself down the steep edge, and going toward the water. Pancho started to leap after him, thought better of it, and raced up and down, barking loudly. He finally found a place where he could run down, and he joined Little Jim. The boy tossed a cake of dry mud into the stream. Pancho dashed into the water after it and finding nothing, bit at the water. He leaped up and down, barking happily and begging Little Jim to toss something that he could get his teeth into and bring out. Little Jim tossed another cake of mud, which Pancho caught in his mouth. It broke up, and Pancho had nothing but a mouthful of dirt. He coughed and shook his head from side to side. Little Jim laughed.

"I am very sorry, Don Francisco," apologized Little Jim. "I did not mean for you to catch that dirt in your mouth. I do not seem to find a stick around here to throw for you."

But Pancho had had enough of this. He came out of the water in long jumps, ran toward Little Jim, spread his feet, and gave himself a mighty shake. The water showered on Little Jim.

"You bad dog!" cried Little Jim, wiping the muddy water from his face. Then he laughed. Pancho romped and played about him, hoping

he would toss a stick into the water. But Little
Jim said, "I do not like your way of playing. We
will go there and sit on the bank and wait for
el capitán. He will come from over there."

He pointed across the stream. Pancho, seeing
the movement of his arm, thought he had thrown
something and dashed toward the water. But he
halted at the edge. Nothing fell. He looked around,
surprised, his mouth grinning, his tail wagging.

"Come, Don Francisco," called Little Jim. "But
keep away from me, you wet, dirty dog."

Pancho followed him up the bank. Little Jim
sat down, pulled a stem of grass, and put it into
his mouth. Pancho lay down beside him.

Lieutenant Baylor and the Rangers returned to
Ysleta late that afternoon. They had chased Victorio and his band of Apaches into the mountains
of Chihuahua in Mexico and then had lost them.
The wily old chief knew the mountains too well
and had hidden so no one could find him.

Pancho liked Lieutenant Baylor at once. He was
a tall, handsome man who spoke softly but with
firmness. Pancho knew by the way Lieutenant
Baylor laid his hand on his head, a strong but
gentle hand, that this was a man he could respect.

"This is a very fine dog," Lieutenant Baylor said. He did not make a fuss over Pancho, but merely laid his hand on him and called him a fine dog. Then he walked away.

At supper, while everyone sat around the table, Lieutenant Baylor listened to the story of Jack Andrews and Bill Wiswald and learned that they were going to San Antonio. He advised them to take the route which led toward Fort Davis where there were United States soldiers, but the two miners wanted to go along the old stage route to the north, as they had some business in New Mexico.

"While I believe most of the Apaches are down in Mexico right now," said Lieutenant Baylor, "there are scattered bands up north. I don't think you will be safe taking that northern route."

"Well, we've got a couple of fine guns, and we're both good shots," said Jack Andrews. "Then, too, we've got Pancho, and he'll soon let us know if any Apaches are around." He looked toward Pancho as he spoke. He said the word "Apaches" rather loudly, and Pancho gave a low growl, looked about, and then got up and wagged his tail and walked over beside Jack Andrews. "Only thing is—" continued Jack, and he smiled— "I hate to part Pancho and Little Jim. They've hit it off so well together. It's like they'd known each other all their lives."

Jack winked at his partner, who nodded his head and grinned.

"Yes," said Bill, "we were thinking that maybe we could take Little Jim along. We could put him in school at San Antonio. He's a bright boy, and he should have a chance at an education."

Lieutenant Baylor laughed. "Did you mention this to Jim Gault?" he asked. "Jim's got something of a fatherly interest in that boy."

"Yes, we spoke to Jim," replied Jack. "He's willing."

"Well, I said I thought it might be a good idea," Jim said, lowering his eyes so as not to meet the gaze of Little Jim, who was sitting across the table from him. "I sort of mentioned it to Little Jim, and I expect he kind of likes the idea." Jim Gault pushed a piece of meat around on his plate. "Sure will miss him, though."

All eyes turned toward Little Jim, who was also looking down at his plate. His face was without expression. No one could tell whether he was sad or happy at the suggestion. He felt he must not show his feelings to anyone, so he simply said, "Big Jim, he thinks it is best. I will go."

"Aw, now come on," urged Jim Gault. "It ain't

like that at all. You don't have to leave unless
you plumb wants to. . . . Anyway, it won't be
long. We'll be back in Santone after a while."

"I would . . . I would like . . ." faltered Little Jim.

If Little Jim showed no signs of being happy
about going, he could not conceal his feelings
from Pancho. The dog seemed to understand. He
went to Little Jim and sat down beside him, his
mouth open in a big grin. Little Jim patted him;
Pancho's tail thumped the floor.

"Guess that settles it," sighed Jim Gault.

After supper Little Jim and Pancho went for
a walk. That is, Pancho went for a walk, and Little
Jim followed. The cook had given Pancho a large
bone after supper. He wanted the bone all right,
but he had no use for it right then, for during
the meal Little Jim had been taking scraps from
his plate and feeding them to Pancho when no
one was looking. So Pancho was not hungry, and
he wanted to hide his bone in a place where he
could find it later. Then, too, as anyone knows,
a bone buried in the ground becomes softer after
a time, and it is more easily chewed. It has a
better taste after it has mellowed in the ground,
too.

Pancho, the bone between his teeth, his head

high and his tail curled, trotted down the narrow street toward the edge of the pueblo. There was no place in the pueblo to bury a bone. The houses had no front or back yards, just hard-packed dirt streets, so he would have to find some place outside the pueblo to deposit his bone.

Little Jim went along to see what Pancho would do. And while Pancho wanted to hide his bone, he apparently trusted Little Jim, and he made no attempt to evade him.

At the last house of the pueblo, just as Pancho was about to go around the corner, a man appeared. He and Pancho almost ran into each other. The man leaped back. Pancho dropped his bone, braced himself as if to spring, and growled.

Little Jim knew the man. He was Jack One Day, the Apache scout. Little Jim guessed he was friendly. He had never given the matter any thought. He just accepted Jack One Day because the Rangers seemed to trust him.

"Watch out!" Little Jim shouted when he saw Jack One Day directly in Pancho's path and noticed the way Pancho acted.

But after leaping back, Jack One Day decided he was not going to let a mere dog block his path. He raised a weighted quirt in his hand.

"Don't hit him!" called Little Jim, starting to-

ward Pancho. "Don Francisco!" he cried. "Come here! Come here!"

But Jack One Day, cursing, struck out with the quirt. Almost at the same time Pancho leaped. The quirt handle struck him on the shoulder and knocked him to the side. Jack One Day did not wait to see what happened. He ran to the door of the house, pushed it open, darted inside, and slammed the door shut.

Pancho was right behind him. He leaped and all four feet struck the door. But it did not open. Growling, Pancho jumped back, feet spread, the

hair on his back and neck standing straight up. Then he ran back and forth in front of the door.

Inside there were loud voices. Little Jim, unafraid, caught Pancho around the neck and began to talk to him softly. Pancho quieted down. He looked at the door and growled again; then, looking at Little Jim, he whimpered. He seemed to be saying, "Just let me get inside that door!"

"No, no, Don Francisco," said Little Jim. "Pay no attention to that man. You come with me."

Then Little Jim called out loudly. "It is all right. I will take Don—the dog away. Do not worry."

Finally getting Pancho away from the door, Little Jim took him to where he had dropped his bone. Pancho started to pick it up, then turned toward the adobe house and growled. Then Little Jim picked up the bone and held it out to Pancho, who took it in his mouth, still growling.

As they walked away Pancho stopped now and then and turned back to look toward the house. Little Jim noticed that he limped slightly when he walked. He began to rub Pancho's shoulder. "That bad man struck you," he said soothingly. "But, my friend, you frightened him. He meant no harm. We will forget about that man."

But Pancho did not appear sure about forgetting the man. Even when they got to a place where he could bury his bone, he still growled to himself. Little Jim watched him as he dragged the earth over the buried bone. Then he laughed. "I hope you remember where you have buried this fine bone, Don Francisco. And do not forget to dig it up early tomorrow. You will never have another chance, for tomorrow we will leave."

If he understood, Pancho paid no attention. He had never buried a bone that he failed to dig up again. He would have this one, too, never fear.

4. On the Trail

THE BONE Pancho had buried and the encounter he had had with Jack One Day seemed to have been forgotten the next morning. At any rate, Pancho considered the bone safe, and Jack One Day was not around to remind him of what had happened the night before.

Besides, Pancho had a lot to do. He had to see that the two horses were properly hitched to the ambulance. He strode around looking things over, sniffing at a girth when it was fastened, seeing that the traces were secured to the singletrees, walking back and forth beneath the two horses, the hair on his back rubbing their bellies and making them snort and prance about.

"Call this dog off!" cried Bill Wiswald. "He's in the way."

Jack Andrews called Pancho, who then went over to see that Jack was fastening his saddle properly. He reared up, placed his forepaws on the pony's withers, and looked things over.

"Down, Pancho!" shouted Jack, turning around, the girth end in his hand. "Where's Little Jim? Call him and get him to take care of this dog."

"Pancho always acts that way when we start," said Bill. "He's anxious to get going."

Just then Little Jim came out of the adobe house. He had a small bundle in one hand and a bow and a quiver of arrows in the other. Pancho raced up to him and almost knocked Little Jim down.

"Don Francisco!" cried Little Jim.

Pancho sniffed the bow. He leaped back, forefeet almost flat on the ground, his haunches high, his mouth in a sort of grin. He barked.

"He sees that bow and thinks you are going hunting," laughed Bill. "Anyway, do something to keep him from under our feet."

Pancho darted away from Little Jim. He stopped and turned, waiting; then he darted off again. He seemed to expect Little Jim to follow him. He would scare up a molly cottontail in no time.

Pancho watched Little Jim go to the ambulance and place his bundle inside. When he saw Little Jim also lay down his bow and quiver, Pancho could not believe it. Finally he walked back slowly toward the boy, as if disappointed.

"That's all right, we'll go hunting, Don Francisco—you and me," Little Jim assured him.

Lieutenant Baylor came out of the house to talk to Jack and Bill. Pancho sat on his haunches and watched, looking from one to the other. Would they stand there talking all day? The other Rangers came out one by one, stretching and yawning. It was hardly daylight.

"Well, I guess we'd better get started," finally called Jack Andrews, walking toward his pony and preparing to mount. He looked at Little Jim. "Do you want to ride in the ambulance, or would you rather ride up behind me for a while?" he asked.

Little Jim, still glancing about him as if he had forgotten something and did not know what it was, appeared not to hear, and Jack had to repeat the question.

"No, I would like to walk with Don Francisco—I mean Pancho," Little Jim then answered.

"Very well, but when you get tired you can

ride, you know," said Jack. He wheeled his horse and started to take the lead.

The boy ran over to Lieutenant Baylor. "Have you seen him?" he asked.

Lieutenant Baylor evidently knew who Little Jim meant by "him."

"Oh, you mean Jim Gault," he said, laughing. "Well, he should be here right now. I let him go up to El Paso last night. . . . He should have been back before now."

Little Jim hesitated, unable to understand Jim Gault's going away without giving him a parting word. He felt very sad about this, but he would not show it. Even if he were an Indian and Indians did not pay much attention to such things as saying good-bye or even hello, Little Jim had thought Jim Gault as a white man would come and say something about having a good trip, or about seeing him later in San Antonio.

"You have a good trip, Jim," Lieutenant Baylor said, placing his hand on Little Jim's head. Then he added, "Jim Gault will catch up with you before you are too far away."

Jim Gault was going with them then! Little Jim walked away and Pancho saw him, jumped up, and ran to his side.

They were ready to leave. Bill Wiswald slapped

the reins on the backs of the horses. The wheels
of the ambulance began to creak.

Just then a horseman came down the street at
a gallop. It was Jim Gault. He reined in his horse
in front of Little Jim and then slid to the ground.
He had a rifle in his hand. "Pretty nearly missed
you," he said. "I went up to El Paso to get you
something."

As Jim held out the rifle the boy's eyes grew
big. A rifle for him!

"Take it, sonny," said Jim Gault. "It's a twenty-
two caliber, just your size. And here, I got you
some ammunition."

Little Jim took the shiny rifle in his hands. He
turned it over and over, looking at it admiringly.

Jim Gault grinned sheepishly. He glanced nervously at his comrades, expecting them to laugh
at him. But they were grinning broadly.

"Had a hard time getting that storekeeper to
open up and sell me this rifle," explained Jim
Gault. "That's why I didn't get back sooner. But
I made it, didn't I?"

"Yes," said Little Jim. He looked at the rifle
and then at Jim Gault. For a moment it seemed
that he would show how he actually felt even
though this would have embarrassed him before
the others.

"It is a fine rifle," he said in a controlled voice. "I will keep it always and will shoot many Apaches with it."

"Don't forget to shoot a few turkeys and squirrels," reminded Jim Gault with a grin. He was relieved that Little Jim had not shown his true feelings. The other Rangers might have laughed.

But Pancho did not care about all this. He showed just how *he* felt. When Little Jim took the rifle in his hands and brought it up to his shoulder and sighted along the barrel, Pancho dashed away in the direction the rifle was pointed, then stopped and looked back to wait for the report of the gun, prepared to dash off in search of whatever Little Jim shot. But when Little Jim took the rifle from his shoulder without shooting, Pancho showed his disgust. He walked back slowly. He would never be able to understand such behavior. A rifle was for hunting—shooting things. He was ready. What was the matter now?

Pancho stood beside Little Jim, glancing up at him, expecting him to raise the rifle once more. But Little Jim stood a moment, his shoulders thrown back, looking at Jim Gault. This man had saved his life. He had treated him like a son. He had just given him a nice new rifle.

But Jim Gault had no more to say, or if he did, he did not say it.

Little Jim went to the ambulance and got out his bow and quiver of arrows. He walked toward Jim Gault, holding the bow and arrows out to the older man. "I have nothing to give in return but these," he said. "You take them."

Jim Gault laughed uncomfortably. He started to reach out, then he dropped his arm, shuffled his feet, lowered his head, and pushed his hat back. He acted, as he might have put it, "plumb embarrassed."

Pancho, standing close to both of them, looked from one to the other. He whimpered. What he meant was "Let's get going. Take those things and stop all this nonsense. We are losing time."

"No, youngster, you keep those things," Jim Gault said after a while. "I don't have any use for them at all. I just wanted you to have that rifle. . . . You run along and I'll be seeing you in Santone."

It looked for a moment as if Little Jim were going to forget he was an Indian, and that he must never show his feelings. He had been taught not to show joy, or grief, or sadness. He stood undecided. Then he reached out and took his friend's hand and squeezed it. Jim Gault swallowed hard.

Little Jim turned and walked toward the ambulance.

Well, that was over! They were ready to go. Pancho barked gaily and romped ahead.

Just then a Ranger walked up to Lieutenant Baylor and said something to him in a low tone. Lieutenant Baylor turned and spoke to several others, and they all shook their heads.

Having turned to wave a good-bye, Jack Andrews saw that something was wrong. He wheeled his horse and rode back to Lieutenant Baylor. Pancho, who had gone some distance up the road, stopped and waited. What was the matter now?

"Something the matter?" Jack asked.

"Nothing that concerns you," said Lieutenant Baylor. "I have just been told that one of our Apache scouts is missing. Not only that, but three of our ponies are gone, too. It looks mighty strange." He turned to the Ranger who had first told him the news. "Maybe he took them to the spring up there. Did you look there?"

"Yep, looked all around . . . no sign of him," replied the Ranger.

Little Jim walked back to stand beside Lieutenant Baylor. "Was it—was it Jack One Day?" he asked.

"Yes, it was Jack One Day," said Lieutenant Baylor. "Do you know anything about him?"

"I know that last night he was here," said Little Jim. "I know that he was unkind to Don Francisco and Don Francisco was angry——"

"Don Francisco?"

"He means Pancho—Pancho the dog," explained Jack, smiling in spite of the seriousness of the situation.

"Well, what happened?" asked Lieutenant Baylor.

"Jack One Day hit Don Francisco with his loaded quirt," said Little Jim, looking at Pancho. Noticing the look and seeing that after all there was some delay, Pancho walked slowly back toward the group.

"That dog didn't like that Injun," growled Jim Gault. "He couldn't understand that Jack One Day was a friendly Apache——"

"Maybe he understood better than we did," cut in Lieutenant Baylor. He laid his hand on Little Jim's shoulder. "Go on. What happened?"

"Don Francisco had a bone he wanted to bury," said Little Jim solemnly. "I went with him. Don Francisco and Jack One Day then came one upon the other, face to face. Without waiting, Jack One

Day raised his quirt and struck at Don Francisco. He hurt his shoulder. But before Don Francisco could get to him, Jack One Day ran into an adobe house and shut the door."

"That's what's wrong," said Jim Gault. "That pesky Injun just cleared out because he was afraid of this dog. He'll come back when the dog's gone."

"And bring your pinto pony, too?" asked the Ranger who had told about Jack One Day's disappearance.

"My pony!" cried Jim Gault. "You mean he took Glass Eye? Well, rattlesnakes and tarantulas—I'll go after that Injun myself!"

"But why not wait?" said Lieutenant Baylor. "You said he'd come back."

"Not if he ran off with Glass Eye!" said Jim Gault, kicking angrily at a pebble. He muttered, "Never did trust that Injun."

Lieutenant Baylor could not keep from smiling. Then he grew serious. "If he ran away, he probably went across the border. We'll see if we can find his trail."

Pancho did not look happy. His tail was hanging down, and he looked quickly from one face to the other. Had he done something wrong?

"Perhaps we better help you," suggested Jack

Andrews. "Pancho here might be able to pick up the trail. We can wait a day or so."

"No," said Lieutenant Baylor. "You go along as fast as you can while Victorio and his warriors are over the border. I suspect they'll be back on this side of the river before long. If you delay, you'll meet up with them or they'll meet up with you. We can handle this."

Jim Gault still was muttering. "I'll give twenty-five dollars to anyone who brings back Glass Eye," he said. "That's a right-smart pony; there's not another like him west of the Pecos . . ."

"We'll find him," said Lieutenant Baylor. He turned to Jack Andrews. "You will be going along the northern route. You might by chance run into Jack One Day. We'll take a look along both sides of the border here." He smiled. "It'll be worth your while now to capture Jack One Day and get Jim Gault's pony—twenty-five dollars reward, you know."

"I'm makin' it thirty!" exclaimed Jim Gault.

Pancho was glad to be back on the trail once more. He took the lead, as usual, and now he had a companion, Little Jim, who seemed to be just as happy as he was. The two kept well ahead of Bill Wiswald, who drove the ambulance, and Jack Andrews, who followed on his pony.

"Perhaps we will pick up Jack One Day's trail," Little Jim told Pancho.

Pancho darted on and off the trail, which led

north and then east. He wanted to see what was behind this big boulder, and what was among that clump of cedar trees. After his side trips he came back, nuzzled and sniffed Little Jim to be sure the boy was all right, then stopped and looked back to see that everything was in order and that the horses were following along properly.

The road led over mountainous country, now going down between two mountains, later winding along the rim of another one. Yucca dotted the landscape; rocks tumbled here and there in piles as if carelessly thrown by some giant hand; the dark red-and-yellow earth glared under the hot January sun.

As the small party made its way along the old road, where boulders had rolled from the heights above, Pancho's keen nose picked up many scents. Some of them caused him to hesitate and growl. He sniffed a track of an ocelot, a catlike animal; or a peccary, a saber-toothed wild hog; wolves had traveled this trail. Pancho barked at an armadillo, an armored creature.

They traveled all day, and by evening arrived at the first old stage station east of El Paso. These stage stations were always about twenty-five miles apart, and it was at such places that the horses were changed and the passengers given a rest, when the stage line was using this route. This station was Hueco Tanks, called Waco Tanks by the old-timers.

5. Pancho Encounters an Apache

Pancho and Little Jim led the way toward the cleared, level space in the center of the great pile of rocks known as Hueco Tanks. Every so often Pancho stopped, raised his nose, and sniffed. Catching the faint scent of something that disturbed him, he gave a short growl each time and then went on. Little Jim's keen glance darted here and there. He peered at the tops of the rocks, into the crevices, and looked carefully at the trail before him. Pancho's actions made him all the more wary. He knew Pancho scented some danger.

"What is it, Don Francisco?" Little Jim asked

as Pancho stopped once more. This time Pancho's hair began to bristle on his neck, and his growl was deeper and more angry. He stood, his nose pointed at something just above his head, jerking his nose up as he sniffed.

Little Jim saw what it was that interested Pancho. It was a small piece of buckskin, caught on the jagged edge of a rock. Little Jim reached up, took it in his hand, and held it toward the dog.

"You smell it," he said to Pancho, who sniffed the buckskin and then snapped at it angrily. Little Jim jerked his hand back just in time. He ran back toward the oncoming ambulance, holding the buckskin out so Bill Wiswald could see it. "This is Apache," he said. "It is from an Apache legging."

Bill drew the reins and brought the horses to a stop. He reached out and took the piece of leather. "How do you know it's Apache?" he asked, examining it. "It looks like a piece of fringe from something all right, but I can't see how you can tell it's Apache."

"Don Francisco knows," said Little Jim. "His nose tells him it's Apache."

Jack Andrews rode up and wanted to know what was wrong. He was shown the piece of buckskin and told what Little Jim had said. "Could have been torn off a legging when a horseman rode by the rock," he said. "And if both Little Jim and Pancho say it's Apache, I guess it must be. We'll have to keep a sharp lookout." He gazed about him. "This would be a fine place to ambush anyone. Plenty of Indians could hide among these rocks and jump out before you knew it."

Jack looked at the buckskin again, shook his head, and then placed the leather in his vest pocket. Bill slapped the reins on the backs of the horses, and they moved ahead.

"We'll be all right in this place," called Bill as they entered the level, walled place in the mass of rocks.

"Yes, it's a natural fort," replied Jack. "I guess we could hold off a bunch of Apaches."

"I hope we don't have to. Anyway, Pancho and Little Jim might be wrong about the presence of Apaches. I don't think they would be in this area. Lieutenant Baylor said we would probably not have to worry until we were several days on the road."

"Well, it won't hurt to be prepared," said Jack. He got down from his pony and took off the saddle and blanket. He tied the pony to a wagon wheel while he helped Bill unharness the two horses at the ambulance.

Meantime, Pancho and Little Jim were busy

looking around. Pancho knew now that they would camp here for the night, and he wanted to be sure everything was safe. He gave every foot of ground a careful smelling, and did not appear to like what his nose told him. Yes, the Apaches were here not so long ago, he seemed to say.

"The Rangers said we could find plenty of water here," said Jack. "Just look around at the holes in these rocks. They catch all the rain water."

"That's why they call it Hueco Tanks, I expect," said Bill. "*Hueco* is the Spanish word for 'hole.'"

They began to look around and soon found fresh rain water that had collected in the holes or tanks in the big rocks. They were surprised at the amount of water stored there, for the rain and weather had formed great bowls in the rocks over a period of thousands of years. There were shallow caves, too, and in some places there were also canyons, which were overhung by roofs and were fine places for shelter.

"We won't have to pitch our tent tonight," said Jack when he found a dry, comfortable gully, roofed in by an overhanging slab of rock.

Scouting about the enclosure, Pancho found several trails which he followed. He ran along, his nose to the ground, and then stopped for Little

Jim to catch up with him. Each time he would give a low growl. "Apache!" Little Jim said, and patted him on the head.

Pancho found a nice, cool bowl of water which had been shaded by an overhanging ledge. The water had flowed in from a larger bowl. Pancho approached it and started to drink. Then he sprang back. Little Jim ran up to him.

"Apache drink here," he said. "We won't drink, eh, Don Francisco?"

Pancho stood and barked at the water as if he expected his enemy to rise from it suddenly.

"Come on!" said Little Jim. "We will find another water hole."

They found one a short distance away, and each took a refreshing drink. Soon the odor of cooking bacon came to them. Jack and Bill had built a small fire and were cooking supper. Little Jim and Pancho thought now they had scouted around enough, and they went to have supper.

Little Jim told the men how Pancho had acted. "He smells plenty of Apaches around here," the boy said. "He smells them on the ground and even at the place they took a drink. The smell is fresh, and Don Francisco does not like it."

"I guess we will have to be careful tonight," said

Jack. "As soon as supper is over we will put out this fire and then tie the horses to the wagon wheels and sleep close to them. Pancho will give us warning if anybody comes near."

"Yes, Don Francisco will let us know," said Little Jim, helping himself to some bacon and potatoes. He sat down with his back to a rock, and ate. Pancho, stretched out beside him, was not worried about his supper. He knew that his friend would leave him plenty on the plate. Little Jim always took enough for both of them.

But Pancho was very hungry and he turned his head now and then toward the plate and then looked at Little Jim. The boy said, "You do not have to wait, Don Francisco. I will feed you as I eat."

He took a rasher of bacon and held it before Pancho's nose. Pancho looked at Little Jim to be sure he understood, and seeing that he could have the bacon, he turned his head slightly sideways and caught the bacon in his mouth. He gulped once and the bacon was gone. His tail beat on the ground.

"You do not chew," scolded Little Jim. "You just swallow that chunk of bacon. If I gave you the whole plate, it would be gone in a moment."

Little Jim looked steadily at Pancho, who looked back at him with big brown eyes which sparkled with anticipation. Pancho knew that such scolding meant nothing, and afterward he would receive another piece of bacon. Sure enough, Little Jim shrugged his shoulders as if it was useless to try and change Pancho. Lifting a strip of bacon from his plate, he held it before Pancho's nose. Snap! The bacon disappeared. Pancho licked his chops. His look made it clear that he wanted more.

"Here, you greedy one—take it all."

There were several slices of bacon and some corn bread on the plate. Hardly had the plate been placed before Pancho than the bacon and corn bread were gone! Then he leisurely licked the plate clean, after which he sank on his haunches and looked at Little Jim.

Pancho was not going to sleep that night, for now that they were once more on the trail he knew it was his duty to protect his masters, as dogs always had to protect all masters. They needed someone to look out after them. They never did seem to have the least idea they were heading straight into danger, and probably just started out, taking the shortest and easiest way. It did not

matter what was in their path. The only time
they knew they were in danger was when danger
was right upon them.

Now Pancho could scent danger a long way off.
By a whiff at the ground he could tell the direction
his enemies were taking. A breeze brought him
all sorts of information—not only scents, but also
sounds which his keen ears picked up and recognized. An enemy might be within a few feet of
them, but if he were quiet and did not show himself, Jack Andrews and Bill Wiswald would pass
right along without noticing. Even a small puppy
would not be so helpless!

Pancho simply could not let them go anywhere
alone; they needed his protection at all times. There
was no telling what trouble they would get into.
Even sometimes when he tried to warn them they
did not understand.

Little Jim was different. He understood Pancho.
Just as when they arrived at this place and Pancho
scented his deadly enemy, the Apache, Little Jim
had understood right away. Jack and Bill might
have thought Pancho was acting the way he did
because there was a rattlesnake curled up in the
rocks, or because he smelled a wolf off in the distance. Not Little Jim; he knew at once.

Pancho, his head resting on his forepaws, looked fondly at Little Jim, who was curled up in a blanket beneath the ambulance. It was dark under there, but Pancho could see him. Little Jim was lying on his right side, his arms doubled up and his head resting on both his hands. His shiny new rifle lay alongside him. He lay very quiet, breathing easily and regularly.

Near-by, under the shelter of the overhanging rock where Jack and Bill were sleeping, came the sound of heavier breathing and an occasional snore. The horses stood, tied to the wheels of the ambulance. Their tie ropes were long enough so that they could lie down if they wished, but all three stood, stomping their feet and blowing. They were restless. Well, horses could smell and hear; they were not as helpless as human beings.

Pancho suddenly pricked his ears. One of the horses gave a low whinny, and Pancho rose to all fours. He stood a moment, his ears flicking back and forth to pick up the slightest sound from any direction, his nostrils working, his eyes trying to pierce the darkness.

Something was moving up the trail. It made a very faint sound, but it was one to be investigated. Pancho went into action, slinking along, hugging the rock wall, in the direction of the sound. Now and then he stopped, one forefoot lifted, as he sniffed and listened. He could smell nothing, but he could hear sounds of movement. He continued along, a silent black figure in the night.

Pancho could hear the sounds plainly now. He recognized them to be the soft sounds of moccasined feet. The wearer of the moccasins was moving carefully, placing each foot down easily to be sure that it did not touch a twig or a loose pebble before he placed his full weight on it.

Pancho soon detected the unmistakable odor of an Apache. As the scent came to him the hair rose on his neck and back. He growled deep inside his throat, a growl that only made a slight gurgle, since he tried to keep it back; it almost made him cough.

Pancho's impulse was to dart forward, take his enemy by surprise, and tear him to pieces. Foam flecked from his mouth.

The sounds were becoming plainer and the odor stronger. Pancho crouched in a crevice of a rock and waited. He would let his enemy come to him. Then he would spring upon him.

The Apache moved closer, picking his way carefully, intent on surprising the white men and coming on them before they could awaken. Probably all he wanted were the horses, but he must cut them loose before their owners realized what was happening. He might even steal away without awakening the men. That would make his feat even more notable when he recounted it to his tribe. Horse-stealing was a fine art with an Apache. . . .

The Indian stopped suddenly. His senses were almost as keen as Pancho's. He could not smell Pancho, as the light breeze was blowing from his rear; he could not see Pancho, who was part of the night himself, and who was half-hidden in the rock crevice. But the Indian sensed some immediate danger. His instinct told him to be careful. He stood still, listening, making no sound.

Pancho waited. The Indian did not move. Pancho still could not see him in the darkness, but he knew exactly where he was; he knew just how far away he was. He waited. Still no sound was heard. Pancho could wait no longer. With a mighty spring he landed in the middle of the trail, bounding in the direction of his enemy.

The Indian heard the sound instantly. Without waiting, he turned and speedily fled in the direction he had come. The Indian leaped upon his horse, who was standing near-by, wheeled him around, and dug his heels into his flank. Pancho was right behind him, and as the horse wheeled, Pancho leaped. The horse shied. Pancho missed the rider, but twisting his head, he snapped his jaws shut and caught the Indian's buckskin shirt in his teeth.

Pancho landed on the ground, rolled over and over, and then gained his feet, but by then the horse was racing up the trail. Pancho started after him, but after going a short distance he slowed down and then stopped. He had not caught the Indian, but he had chased him away. Now he must get back to camp.

Pancho still had a piece of the Indian's shirt between his teeth when he arrived back at the ambulance. Everything was peaceful there. Little Jim did not appear to have moved since Pancho had gone. The heavy breathing and snores of the men could be heard from beneath the rock shelter. The horses seemed quieter, and one had even lain down.

Giving his head a little toss, Pancho opened his teeth at the same time, and the piece of torn buckskin fell to the ground near Little Jim. Settling down beside the boy, Pancho listened for a time, sniffed the air several times, and then with a sigh began to lick the white streak on his side.

6. An Ambush

WHEN LITTLE JIM awoke the next morning the first thing he saw was Pancho, whose brown eyes were gazing directly at him. It was daylight and Little Jim was surprised that he had slept through the night without once awakening. But he had been very tired, having walked a long distance the day before.

He thought Pancho's long, earnest look was trying to express disapproval at his sleeping so soundly. "You seem to scold me, Don Francisco, with those big eyes of yours," said Little Jim, yawning. "But I slept soundly, knowing that you

79

would be on guard and no one would be able to
come near our camp."

Pancho's gaze became more intense. Seeing that
he had Little Jim's attention, Pancho dropped his
eyes to the piece of buckskin that had dropped the
night before beside the sleeping Indian boy. Little
Jim looked down, following Pancho's gaze. He saw
the buckskin. "Ah, you have taken that buckskin
from Don Juan and placed it before me to remind
me that there is danger here," he said. Then he
reached out and picked up the buckskin. "No," he
said, "this is not the same piece you and I found
hanging from that rock. Where did you get it?"

Pancho, who had been lying down, quickly got
to his feet. Then he turned and ran a short distance, stopped, and looked back at Little Jim. He
gave a quick bark, and turned and ran a little
farther, stopping and turning toward Little Jim
once more.

"I see," said Little Jim, throwing off his blanket
and getting up. "You want me to follow you. You
will show me where you found this buckskin."

Pancho's bark had aroused Jack Andrews and
Bill Wiswald, who came out from beneath the
rock shelter. "What's the trouble here?" called Jack.
"What's Pancho barking at?" He did not think

it was too important, for he stood and lifted his arms above his head and gave a big yawn.

"Pancho thinks we should be up and moving," said Bill. "I guess he is right. It's already daylight."

Little Jim walked toward them, holding the piece of buckskin. "Don Francisco brought this to me while I slept," he said.

"How did he get it out of my pocket?" said Jack in surprise. Reaching in his jacket pocket, his hand came out with the other piece of buckskin. A puzzled expression came over his face. Then he grinned. "Oh, so he found another piece, did he?"

"No," said Little Jim. "The pieces are not the same. That one you have is dark; it was tanned by the smoke of the old white cedar. This one" —he held out the piece in his hand—"is yellow and was tanned by the smoke of the young white cedar."

"They *are* a different color," agreed Bill.

"Well, that just means two Indians, instead of one, were here before we came," said Jack. "We'd better feed and water the horses and get on our way."

Bill thought so, too, but Pancho had different ideas. Now that everyone was awake and up, he believed they should start out at once after the Indian who had come upon their camp the night before. Little Jim realized that Pancho was anxious to go along the trail toward the east, but he explained, "That is the way we are going, Don Francisco, after we have had breakfast and hitched the horses to that wagon. So do not be in such a great hurry. If there is anyone down that trail who is not friendly to us, we shall see him. You are trying to warn us, so now we shall be on the watch."

Little Jim gave Pancho a pat on the back and went to help with the morning chores. He had to build a fire so they could have coffee and bacon. But Pancho did not go with him to collect firewood. Instead, he paced up and down the road, smelling here and there. He sat on his haunches and whined, turning his head to see if the others were not yet ready.

Finally, breakfast over, the horses fed and watered and hitched to the ambulance, Bill got into the driver's seat and Jack mounted his pony. Little Jim refused to ride and said he would walk along with Pancho as he had the day before.

When Pancho saw they were going in the direction he wanted to go, he barked his joy and raced ahead. He had picked up the trail of the Indian, and by the time they reached Hueco Pass, a high wall of rock with the Hueco Mountains on one side and Cerro Alto on the other, he began to race back and forth along the narrow road. He ran forward with his nose to the ground; then he ran back, bounding up and down in front of Little Jim and finally darting away to give Little Jim the idea he must follow quickly. "Don Francisco is very excited about something," Little Jim called to Jack.

"He wants you to follow him," laughed Jack, urging his pony forward alongside Little Jim.

"But I am following him—we are following him," replied Little Jim. "There is no way to go but straight ahead, and it is the way we are going. That is the way Don Francisco wants to go. But he wants to tell us something else."

"Perhaps he wants us to follow faster," called Bill. "He's probably discovered a band of antelope."

"I'll go on ahead with him and see what he's after," said Jack.

"And I will go, too," said Little Jim.

"Then get up here on the pony, behind me," suggested Jack.

"No, I will run. On this ground I can go faster than the pony," said Little Jim. He was right, for the road was very rough. It had gullies which had been cut by water running down from the high walls, and it was covered with fallen rocks and dirt.

Little Jim waved to Pancho, who started ahead. But when he had gone a few hundred yards, Pancho suddenly stopped and trotted back and forth. Then he sat down and turned his nose upward, sniffing as if interested by some scent above him.

Little Jim stopped, too. He looked up. Then he shouted, "Look out!"

Jack reined in his pony just in time. There was a rumbling sound above, followed by a crash. A huge rock fell onto the road just ahead of Jack's pony. This was followed by a rattle of smaller stones and earth.

"Whew! That was a close one," called Jack.

Little Jim ran back to him. "We must get out of this pass quickly," he said. "I am sure that stone was pushed over by those who are not our friends. Don Francisco has smelled them."

"This is a big one," replied Jack, looking at the rock. "Maybe it just broke loose. There are a lot of rocks here which must have fallen of their own accord."

"No, we must get out quickly," Little Jim insisted.

Jack turned his pony and went back to the ambulance. The team had stopped, and Bill was standing beside the ambulance, his rifle at his shoulder.

"What is it—what's the matter?" called Jack.

Bill's reply was a shot. The bullet whined through the air, followed by a rattle of pebbles and earth from above.

"We've got to keep up the fire to get through here," said Bill, lowering his rifle. "Those Indians will kill us by pushing rocks over that cliff. I'm going to lead the two horses and keep shooting as I go along. I think you better get down from your pony and do the same."

"Did you see anything—anyone?" asked Jack, dismounting.

"Well, I'm not sure I saw anyone," replied Bill, "but I saw something move up there, and as that big rock came down I was sure it was pushed over the edge."

Jack drew his own rifle from the saddle scabbard. He carried it in one hand and led his mount by the reins. Both he and Bill looked up as they walked along, watching the tops of both sides of the high rock walls. Neither saw anything suspicious.

"The chances are that the rock was just about ready to fall and was jarred loose by our coming through here," said Jack after they had gone some distance.

"I guess you're right," admitted Bill. "I must have just imagined I saw something move up there—something that looked like an Indian. I've got Indians on my mind."

"But Pancho is excited about something," continued Jack. "That dog must have seen or smelled something that's making him act this way."

"How are we to know what it is?" replied Bill. "Maybe a mountain lion came near the camp last night. Maybe it was a loafer wolf. It could have been any number of animals in these mountains. He just picked up the trail this morning and that's what excited him."

"Yes, that's true. Pancho could find a lot of things in the mountains that he is not familiar with—animals he wasn't likely to meet on the plains."

They walked along in silence.

"He seems to have quieted down," Jack said finally. "He's not running back and forth and whining. He certainly saved my life; I reined in my horse just in time."

"What does Little Jim think?" asked Bill. "If anyone understands that dog, it is the boy. They speak the same language."

"Little Jim thinks Pancho is trying to warn us that Indians—Apaches—are about," said Jack. "But you must remember that both the dog and boy have this common enemy. I would say that whenever they sense danger they are apt to think it is the Apaches."

"Anyway, I guess we'd better be careful," said Bill.

Pancho wanted to get through the pass as quickly as possible. He seemed to have lost the trail. However, he might be able to pick it up at the other end. He knew the Apaches were near. He could not mistake that smell, yet it puzzled him. It seemed to be everywhere. He could not get his nose into a moccasin track or whiff anything an Apache had touched. It was just there—in the air.

"We must not let our masters walk into an ambush, Don Francisco," confided Little Jim, who watched Pancho closely. "We must go on ahead and be sure the way is clear at the other end of this pass. I know that you have smelled out the enemy. I am sure that you found one of them early this morning and that you got a good hold

of him and he escaped. But our masters do not
think so. They believe that you and I think that
every strange sound, every strange smell, every
strange track of any kind is made by an Apache,
because we hate the Apache so much. Is that not
true?"

Pancho turned his head and looked into Little
Jim's eyes. He understands, thought Little Jim. He
knows what I am talking about, and he agrees with
me. He feels sorry that Don Juan and Don Guillermo do not understand.

"So we must protect them," said Little Jim
aloud, slapping Pancho on the haunch. "Go and
find what is ahead. I shall be right behind you.
But you must be careful."

Pancho was careful. He was not going to over-
look anything. He went back and forth across the
road, his nose to the ground, sniffing everywhere.
He stopped and raised his head and sniffed the
air, each sniff bringing his head a little higher. Yes,
the enemy was somewhere; he was in that region
somewhere. But just where, Pancho could not de-
termine.

Having traveled through the pass without any
more trouble, Jack and Bill were more convinced
than ever that the great stone had rolled over the
edge of its own accord. Jack was once more

mounted, his rifle in his scabbard, and Bill had taken his seat on the wagon. They wended their way through the foothills of the Hueco Mountains and then crossed beautiful plains which were thick with antelope. Jack brought one down and that night when they reached Alamo Springs they had fresh meat for supper.

Pancho busily investigated the camp and surrounding area. He knew that Indians had not been in this place for some time, yet he was always on the alert. Every now and then he would go a short distance in the direction they had come, looking and sniffing. Possibly the Indians were trailing them.

The next day they made the third stage station out of El Paso. This site nestled among strange piles of dark granite rocks which towered into the air and was known as Las Cornudas—the Horned Ones. Jack and Bill had been warned by Lieutenant Baylor to be watchful at this station, as it was the favorite watering place of the Apaches from the Tularosa Agency in New Mexico, on their raids into Texas and Mexico. Even though there were Indian signs at this station, Pancho did not appear too excited about them.

On the fourth day, after a thirty-mile trip, they arrived at Crow Flat, also known as Crow Springs.

7. Pancho Left on Guard

Pancho trotted into the old stage station at Crow Flat. Only the thick adobe walls of the station remained, and these were overgrown with wild-grape vines. On one side was a large opening through which stagecoaches were driven in the old days.

Pancho arrived first to be sure that everything was safe for the others. He trotted around the enclosure, poking his nose here and there, scaring up some small birds who had been dusting themselves in a sunny corner. Pancho found nothing suspicious and went back to the entrance where he stood as Little Jim came up, followed by the others.

"We will have our noon meal here, Don Francisco, and perhaps remain until tomorrow," said Little Jim, rubbing Pancho's ears. Pancho whined his approval.

Jack rode in and looked around. He turned in the saddle and shouted to Bill, "Drive right on inside. We can get out of that cold wind and have dinner."

A chill north wind had been blowing all morning, and it was good to get inside the walls in the warm sunshine. Pancho watched the arrival of the ambulance. He saw the horses unhitched, hobbled, and turned out with the saddle pony. Everything met with Pancho's approval. There was no danger; no Indians had been here.

Pancho went over to the north wall, circled around several times in a spot he selected, and then lay down. The sun felt good, and he needed a rest. He crossed his paws, laid his head on them, watched Little Jim start a fire, and finally closed his eyes.

Pancho awoke all at once. He was on his feet, growling, his neck hair bristling. He heard yells, the trampling of horses' hoofs, and gunfire. He

bounded to the entrance as Little Jim shouted, "Down, Don Francisco! Down!"

Little Jim was behind Jack, who had his rifle to his shoulder, firing. On the other side of the entrance, shielded by the wall, Bill also was shooting at something.

Several hundred yards away about ten mounted Indians, circling on their horses, yelling, and shooting their guns, were driving off the two ambulance horses and the saddle pony.

"Keep shooting, Bill," called Jack. "If we can keep them from getting those hobbles off, we might save the horses."

"Our horses don't seem to be worrying about hobbles," replied Bill between shots. "They are frightened enough to make as good time with hobbles on as they would with them off."

Sure enough, the horses were being driven away by the Indians. Even though their front feet were hobbled together they were leaping and jumping wildly forward, the Indians behind them yelling, waving their arms, shooting, and striking at them with their quirts.

Several Indians dropped back and continued to shoot at the adobe stage station. Jack and Bill, seeing their horses disappearing, ran out and continued firing at the Indians.

"We got one!" cried Jack as they saw an Indian topple from his pony.

The riderless pony ran off in the direction of the others, while the other Indians who had dropped back, dismounted and picked up their fallen comrade. They placed him on one of the ponies, and then they all rode away.

Little Jim held tight to Pancho, who several times almost got away, so anxious was he to take off after the Indians.

Jack and Bill came back, leaned their rifles against the adobe wall, and both sank to the ground. They could see, a mile or more to the west, the small band of Indians riding away in triumph.

"Well, what are we going to do now?" asked Jack, removing his hat and wiping the sweat from his forehead.

"We are going to have to think and think hard," replied Bill.

"If we hadn't been such fools, we would have taken the advice of the Rangers and gone along that route to Fort Davis," sighed Jack.

"There's no use worrying about that now."

"No."

Little Jim, still holding on to the loose skin of Pancho's neck, came closer, bringing the dog with him. "I could go for help," he suggested. Both men looked up at him. "Don Francisco and I could go back to the Ranger camp and tell them about the Indians—they would like to know about the Apaches being around here," he continued. Pancho whined as if he understood.

Jack and Bill, both thinking the same thing, looked at each other. Bill spoke. "No, it's a hundred miles back there—you'd never make it. Anyway, Jack and I wouldn't let you do that, would we, Jack?"

"We certainly would not!" agreed Jack. He paused. "You know, Bill, it's only about seventy-five miles to the Pecos River," he said at last. "Don't you think it would be better to go on there, instead of turning back?"

"We would have to carry all our food and water and blankets," said Bill. "And what would we do with all these valuable instruments, this new wagon, our guns, and all these things?"

"Well, we could hide most of the things and take a chance on the rest being here when we returned."

"I don't think it would be wise to go to the Pecos," said Bill. "We're not familiar with the route. We'd have to go through those Guadalupe Mountains. That looks like pretty rough country." He pointed toward the east. In the distance could be seen the outline of the mountain chain, with one tall peak standing out.

"Don Francisco and I could stay here and guard everything while you went back to the Ranger camp," said Little Jim. Pancho, who had sunk down on his belly, listening to the conversation, thumped the ground with his tail and whimpered on hearing his name.

Both men shook their heads. "I've got it!" said Jack. "We can all three go back and leave Pancho here to guard things. We can tie him up on a long rope so he can reach the water, and we'll leave enough food for him——"

"You would leave Don Francisco tied up?" asked Little Jim. "No, if you leave him, he must not be tied up. He could not fight the Apache if he were tied up. He will remain and guard everything if you want it, but he must not be tied up."

Both men looked at Little Jim in surprise. Pancho gave a series of short, happy barks.

"I believe he is right," said Jack, turning to Bill, who nodded. Jack continued, "That dog would never let an Apache get near this place. That is, if he would stay here. I believe he would——"

"Well, he did let them get near today," corrected Bill.

"You can't blame Pancho for that. He gave us plenty of warning that Apaches were on our trail, even way back at Hueco Tanks. It was our own fault for letting those horses wander off. Why, they must have been two or three hundred yards away when the Indians got them. You can't blame Pancho."

"You're right," said Bill. "I'm sorry." He turned to Pancho as he spoke and laid his hand on the dog's head. Pancho had something to say, some explanation to make, but no one could understand him. His thoughts had to be expressed in whines, barks, tail waggings, ear flickings, and growls.

During the afternoon Pancho watched as Jack and Bill worked around the old stage station. He could not understand what they were doing, and as he had been forbidden to go out and pick up the trail of the Indians, he selected a place in the sun, keeping open one eye or the other to be sure he did not miss anything.

First the two men, with the aid of Little Jim, pulled the ambulance farther back into the enclosure. Then they took two burlap bags and filled them with dried grass. After tying up the bags, they placed a cord around each one, near an end.

They shifted the grass around by molding the outside so that each bag had a lump on the end about the size of a man's head. The men took two old hats and placed them on the "heads" of the stuffed bags. Then they placed the bags high up on two poles.

"At a distance they will look like real men," said Jack admiringly.

"I think they should have shoulders," suggested Bill. "Just enough to show over the walls."

So they cut two shorter sticks and lashed them just below the "necks" of the dummies, covering them with two old shirts. Then they leaned the dummies against the walls, one on one side and one on the other.

Jack went outside and walked away a distance. "Looks natural!" he called. Then he came back. "I think we should have some kind of shiny metal on the wall just in front of each one of these dummies—something that will shine in the sun like a gun barrel."

"Let's put those two old Springfield rifles there," suggested Bill.

They went to the ambulance and got out the rifles, placing them on the wall in front of the dummies, the rifle barrels pointing outward.

"The only trouble is that these things can't move," said Jack. "If the Indians come, they'll notice that these dummies don't move even if they shoot at them."

"That's where I think Pancho will come in handy. He'll move around. The Indians will see him, and it will never occur to them that he is alone."

"Pancho? You really think we should leave him here alone?"

"I don't see why not. We can leave him enough food; he will have plenty of water at that spring. He'll have everything he wants."

"But, Bill, think of that dog being here by himself all the time we're gone. That is, if he will stay. I don't think that would be right. Suppose something should happen to us. He'd starve to death. I'd rather lose everything——"

"But nothing's going to happen to us. We'll be back here in a week or ten days. Once we get horses we can return in a couple of days."

Jack studied the matter for a time. "I don't think Little Jim would leave him," he said finally. "He'll either want to stay or take the dog along."

"Well, you know as well as I do that we couldn't leave Little Jim. We've got to protect our property. We've got thousands of dollars worth of equipment here, as well as ammunition and other things. Maybe one of us should stay."

"No, I don't think one man could get through. We'll both have to stay or both go."

The two men stopped talking and looked at Little Jim and Pancho. The boy was leaning down, his face close to Pancho's, and he seemed to be talking to the dog. Pancho's tail was thumping the ground. Now and then he would whine and rub his nose against Little Jim's face.

"You'll have a hard time separating those two," said Jack, gathering up the tools and walking toward the wagon.

"I'll explain to Jim," said Bill. "He can tell Pancho to stay. I believe the dog will mind him."

Pancho watched until all the work was done. The men made their blankets into a roll and placed their supplies in saddlebags to be carried over their shoulders. They took up their rifles.

Little Jim, seeing they were about ready to leave, made last preparations for his friend. He led Pancho to the rear of the ambulance and told him to stand up and look inside. Pancho rested his forepaws on the top of the tailgate.

"There, Don Francisco, is a large piece of bacon,"

said Little Jim. "It is even more than we take
ourselves. It is for you. I leave it in here so that
the small animals do not eat it up. You will drag
it out, but you must guard it. There is a sack of
corn beside the bacon. I do not think that is good
food for a fine dog like you—it was meant for the
horses. And do not forget the large antelope bone
we gave you for lunch."

Pancho looked into the ambulance and then
turned his brown eyes directly on Little Jim. He
whined, seeming to understand the bacon was for
him.

Little Jim now took some sacks, and tossing them
under the ambulance, he said to Pancho, "You
sleep here." To better show what he meant, he
crawled under the ambulance and lay down on
the sacks. "It is nice," he said. "Come!"

Pancho went to him and sat down on the sacks.
He did not seem to understand why Little Jim
was making a bed like this when everyone was
leaving. "Lie down here!" ordered Little Jim.
Pancho lay down beside Little Jim, who leaned
on his elbow and stroked the dog's neck. Pancho
grunted contentedly. But shouldn't they get up
and hurry? Jack and Bill had appeared ready to
leave!

"Jim!" called Jack. "Jim, come on!"

Little Jim patted Pancho again. He placed the dog's head against his own; then he jumped up.

With a glad bark, Pancho jumped up too. He ran ahead of Little Jim. Stopping in front of Jack and Bill, he gave a quick bark and started along the trail. "Don Francisco!" Little Jim's voice rang out. "Don Francisco, come back here!"

Pancho raced back. He ran in a circle around Little Jim. "Here, Don Francisco—down!" ordered Little Jim.

Pancho came toward Little Jim meekly. He squatted on his haunches, his tongue hanging out, looking at his young master.

"Don Francisco, you stay here!" said Little Jim. "Understand? You stay here!"

Pancho gave a little whine and shook his head. Did he understand correctly? Was he ordered to remain behind? Was this a game?

Little Jim patted him. The two men already had started away, and Little Jim turned and went after them. After he had walked several steps he turned and looked back at Pancho. Pancho did not move, but his muscles were tensed. He was ready at the word now to dart ahead. Little Jim was not smiling. His face was sad. It almost looked as if he was going to cry.

Suddenly Little Jim ran back to Pancho. "You be a good dog . . . you stay here . . . you guard everything . . . we will be back. Don Francisco, *I* will be back." He kneeled down and hugged Pancho. Pancho could not understand that peculiar sniffling sound. He had never heard it before.

Little Jim got up quickly and ran after the two men. He did not look back. Pancho sat as he had been told. He did not move. Little Jim had told him to stay. Pancho had thought it was a game, and perhaps it was. But he would wait now until he got the command to follow.

The two men walked on ahead. Little Jim was right behind them. Still he did not turn around. Still he did not whistle. Still he did not call.

Pancho sat looking after the two men and the boy. On they went along the trail. As he watched them he pointed his ears so he could better hear the command to follow. He was set to spring forward. He could catch up with them in two leaps, three leaps—maybe four or five.

But no command came. Pancho's ears fell back. They pointed again. He whined and lifted one forepaw and then the other. His tail rose and fell. He pointed his ears again. He turned his head slightly and looked after the three.

The two men disappeared around a curve in

the trail. Little Jim, who seemed to walk more slowly, almost stopped. But he did not turn around. He did not wave. He did not call. Suddenly he began running and then he, too, was out of sight.

Pancho was all alone.

8. "Don Francisco Will Stay!"

LITTLE JIM did not dare look back. He knew that if he did, he would not be able to keep from raising his hand in a farewell to Pancho. Perhaps, too, he might not be able to go on, for seeing Pancho in the distance, and remembering that look in his eyes which told that he could not believe Little Jim meant for him to remain behind, Little Jim would turn and run back. He would have to take a more affectionate farewell of his friend. Then maybe he would not be able even to leave him this time.

So Little Jim trudged along, behind Jack Andrews and Bill Wiswald, stumbling over stones and slipping into ruts, not watching where he was going. Yet he did not turn his head to look back.

Little Jim hoped Jack and Bill would not look at him. Although it was almost dark, he was sure they would be able to see the expression on his face, an expression he could not control. He felt as if his face, no matter how hard he sought to control it, would give away his feelings. He wanted to run off to the side, hide behind a rock or tree, and wait until he was more able to get control of himself.

The boy did not want anyone to look at him when he felt as he did. Despite the fact that he was an Indian and no Indian should ever let anyone read his grief on his face, he could not trust himself. Back there he had been on the point of crying. When he turned and ran back to Pancho and hugged him the last time he could hardly control himself. He was ashamed that even Pancho had seen him like that. . . .

His upbringing had taught him never to show grief, or to cry out in pain. Well, no pain of any sort would cause him to cry out. Yet no one had ever taught him how he must act when he was forced to leave behind a pet, or rather, a friend like Don Francisco.

The two men led the way, following the trail over which they had traveled earlier that day. They had debated the wisdom of taking the trail, and had decided that it might be better to strike out in a straight line for Ysleta. As they would be traveling at night, however, and there would be no moon until later, they thought it better to take the trail during the first stage of the journey back.

The trail would lead them back to the stage station in the Cornudas Mountains, where they hoped to arrive by dawn. There they would find water, and after a rest, they would then leave the road and strike out over the plains and mountains.

After walking along for several hours they stopped and sat down for a short rest. "Do you think that dog will actually remain there?" asked Jack, voicing the thought that was in both men's minds.

Little Jim firmly answered, "Don Francisco, he will remain there." He believed it, of course. He believed it even more now, since they had gone several miles and Pancho had not come after them. The thought of Pancho there, all alone, not quite understanding why he had been left behind, caused the Indian boy to feel melancholy once more.

"If Pancho is there and keeps moving about, the Indians will see something alive," Jack continued.

"They will think we still are there, hidden from view. Otherwise, why would a dog be there all alone? That's the way they will reason. That is, of course, if Pancho stays there."

"Don Francisco will stay," said Little Jim.

"Well, we had to take that chance," said Bill. "In fact, what else could we do? We couldn't bring all those things with us. We both had to come, so one could not remain on guard. One man couldn't get back to the Ranger camp alone. Now let us hope that Pancho guards things safely until we get back."

"Don Francisco will not leave," said Little Jim.

Jack laughed, reaching over to pat Little Jim's arm. "Of course, we know he will stay there until we get back," he said, getting up. "I think we'd better get on our way."

They started out once more. The moon had not risen, but the stars were out, so they could see the trail. On and on they walked through the night, Little Jim keeping up the rear. He was listening for some sound of Pancho coming after them. Although he would have been disappointed if Pancho had appeared, he half hoped that he would.

The moon rose, making it easier for them to follow the trail. Then, after hours more of walking,

it began to get light. They found themselves in
the midst of a hilly, rocky country. As the dawn
came they hurried on, hoping to make the stage-
coach station in the Cornudas, where they would
rest and get water. Once there, they would decide what route to take back to the Ranger camp.

Pancho sat on his haunches for some time at
the entrance of the stage station, watching the
turn in the trail to the west. He expected to see
Little Jim and his two masters come suddenly into
view at any moment. The wind was blowing the
wrong way, so he was unable to tell anything by
smelling.

Pancho had been told to stay in camp, a command he understood. But what he did not understand was how long he was to remain there. Such
things were not questioned. He only knew that
the order to stay would remain in effect until some
other order was given.

He waited patiently. Finally he let his forelegs
slide forward and he lay down, keeping his head in
the direction Little Jim and his masters had taken.
At the slightest sound—the rustling of a leaf, the
hopping of a bird from branch to branch—he raised
his head, ears pointed and pricked.

Then, with a sigh, he again rested his jowls on his forepaws and watched the trail. Occasionally he looked out over the country to the south. The land sloped down and he could see for miles. There did not seem to be a creature in sight. The antelope, which had been grazing some distance away, had disappeared.

Dusk came and everything was very quiet. Even the wind hardly stirred. At such times sounds could

be heard for long distances. Pancho strained to hear some far-off sound which would tell him that the others were coming back.

The silence of nature made him restless. He got up, opened his mouth wide in a yawn, trotted over to the spring, and lapped up some water. Then he sniffed around to see if there had been any recent visitors to the spring. Finally he went back to his post.

It was getting dark, so he remained there for only a short time. He had to see that everything was in order. First he went around the outside of the wall, sniffing, listening, and looking. He made a tour of the inside of the station. Walking beneath the ambulance and sniffing at the sacks Little Jim had placed there, he whined at the familiar scent. Then he walked out from beneath the vehicle and reared up to peer in the front part of the ambulance. His keen nose detected the familiar odor of horses from the harness which had been left there, and he sniffed the scent of Bill on the seat.

He went to the rear of the ambulance and placed his forepaws on the tailgate. Jack's saddle was right inside, bringing back to Pancho the memory of the saddle pony and Jack. Little Jim, Jack, Bill, and the horses were all here in a way. Their familiar smells made Pancho feel they were here.

Pancho trotted back to the entrance and took another look down the trail. It was too dark to see far, but he smelled nothing, nor did he hear anything which would indicate anyone's approach. He could hear the bubbling of the spring and the lonesome sound of a twittering bird. The bird was twittering in a sleepy, comfortable way as if it were settled for the night and happy.

Once more making the round of the adobe walls, Pancho flushed a molly cottontail. He made a dash in pursuit and then braked himself. The white tuft of a little rabbit's tail bobbed up and down as the frightened creature disappeared in the darkness, but Pancho went back and sniffed around to see what had brought the rabbit there. He could find nothing; it must have been curiosity.

Back at the entrance he sat on his haunches, jerking his head up and down, his nostrils opening and closing as he sniffed the air. His ears flicked back and forth. He could detect many little sounds now, night sounds. Creatures were stirring about him—small, timid creatures who fed at night, afraid to roam during the day.

Pancho was a creature of habit. When night came

he associated it with a quiet camp, the horses
snorting and blowing as they grazed during the
earlier hours, the low voices of men as they talked
over the events of the day and their plans for the
next day. And recently, Little Jim beside him, talking to him in Mexican, or thinking his own thoughts,
his hand idly stroking Pancho at the same time.

Now Pancho found things not just right. He was
all alone in the night. There were no voices, no
sound of horses, no one who placed a caressing
hand upon his back. The absence of such familiar
things disturbed him.

He began to whimper. Something must have
happened to his two-legged friends, who had gone
off alone and left him behind. They depended so
much on him. He did so many things for them.
They could not do without him! But they had—
and see what had happened! They had lost their
way and now could not get back to their camp.
He would have to signal them.

Pancho raised his head, his muzzle pointing upward, his mouth in an O-shape, and howled long
and loudly. Back to him came the echoes until
they died out. Then, out of the night came an
answering howl. A wolf!

Pancho was interested in this. He stared into

the darkness and tried to pick up the wolf's scent. He knew wolves were enemies to him and to the men. His hair bristled, and he gave a series of warning growls.

Now Pancho did not hesitate. Wolves were about, and his friends were in danger. He started on a trot along the way Little Jim and Bill and Jack had gone. His nose was close to the ground and he went straight ahead. It was easy to follow this trail-scent.

He had not gone far before he stopped.

"Don Francisco, you stay here!"

The One-With-the-Soft-Voice had said this. Pancho had been told to remain. No reason was given, and he would not have understood if there had been a reason. He was just told to stay.

Pancho turned about and walked back toward the stage station, his tail drooping, slinking along as if he had done something for which he might be punished. He returned to his post at the entrance and sank on his haunches. Twisting around, he began to lick the line of white hair on his side.

The moon rose. The cedar trees, the adobe wall, the ambulance, the shrub-growth downhill from the stage station, all seemed to stand out in ghostlike whiteness. A howling wolf was answered by another. Pancho's growls blended with the echoes.

Suddenly there was a terrifying scream. It seemed to come from a few yards away. Pancho leaped back, his teeth bared, his hair bristling. A mountain lion! Pancho knew from the faint scent that reached him that the ferocious creature was some distance away. A mountain lion's scream always seems close at hand.

The night was coming to life. Pancho heard noises near the spring, the usual nightly watering place for all the wild creatures in that area. All came stealthily—some merely to drink and escape with their lives, others to drink and prey upon the weaker.

The breeze coming from the spring told Pancho at once that antelope were there. They had not gotten his scent, or they would not have approached so near. Pancho slunk along on his belly, making no noise.

Since this spring was a part of his domain, he was going to decide which animals could use it and which could not. Coming to a stop just behind a bush, he saw two antelope in the moonlight. The large-antlered buck was a noble creature, proud and haughty. He held himself erect, his head high, watching while the doe had her fill. The doe daintily drank the water, now and then throwing her head back to swallow.

These two could drink safely, Pancho decided. He would not chase them away, possibly because he respected the buck's antlers. However, had he been in want of food, he would have thought little of attacking the buck.

Suddenly both antelope leaped into the air and were gone like a flash. At the same time there came the piercing cry of the mountain lion, this time very close to the spring. Pancho leaped to his feet, growling, every hair on his back standing straight up, his teeth bared.

A mountain lion, evidently angered at having missed his prey, appeared, slinking along, his tail thrashing furiously. He was headed in the direction of the spring. This was one fellow who was not welcome.

Pancho crouched, his belly almost touching the ground. He advanced cautiously toward the spring from the other side. The mountain lion got his scent and hesitated. Pancho growled. The lion, screaming again, turned and fled.

Pancho watched him go, his mouth open as if in a grin, his great tongue lolling out the side. He walked to the spring and took a drink. He was not thirsty, but this spring was his and he would drink whenever he liked. He lapped up a few tonguesful of water and then walked back, his tail curled in an arc over his back.

He made a round of the adobe walls, and then went back to his post at the entrance. He lay down, his paws crossed and his jowls resting on them, watching now the spring and now the trail. Soon he heard noises about the spring. When he heard the grunt of a peccary he started to get up and investigate, but sank down again with a sigh.

Wolves howled in the distance. Every once in a while the mountain lion uttered his bloodcurdling scream. The night wore on. At daybreak Pancho was in the same place, watching and waiting.

9. The Fight

"Apaches!" cried Little Jim. They had just come around a bend in the trail. There, before them, were fifty or more Indians. It was an entire village on the move, the braves riding in front, with the pack horses, squaws, and children bringing up the rear.

"They're Indians all right," exclaimed Bill. "And I guess if you say they're Apaches, they must be."

"Come on, let's run!" said Jack.

"No use, for they're mounted and will catch us in no time," said Bill. "We'd better make for that hill."

The braves leading the party had already seen them. With a whoop they started their horses on a run toward them.

The two men and Little Jim left the trail and ran up a gently sloping hill to their left. Making their way around the huge boulders which covered the hill, they reached the top. The summit of the hill was also covered with loose rocks.

"Let's make a breastwork," said Bill. They had hardly started to pile up the rocks when the braves who were racing toward them came to the point where they had left the trail.

Several began shooting, and some of the bullets struck the rocks and glanced off, while others whined overhead. But soon Jack and Bill and Little Jim had enough rocks piled up so they could lie safely behind them.

"Hold your fire," advised Jack. "We'll wait until they charge up the hill."

All at once the Indians stopped shooting. Bill peeped over the top of the pile of rocks before him. "They've vanished," he said. "I don't see one Indian!"

"Yes, even the horses are gone, as well as the pack animals in the rear," said Jack, also looking.

"They have gone down the other side of the

trail," said Little Jim. "They are planning some-thing. We must watch carefully."

"I think we'd better build up this breastwork all around us," suggested Jack.

They began making a circular breastwork of rocks. The hill sloped down evenly on all sides, so they could defend their position in all directions.

"Now, you keep a sharp lookout in the rear, and I'll watch here in front," said Jack. "Jim here can watch first on one side and then on the other. They won't be able to surprise us."

"That's all very well," grumbled Bill. "But how long are we going to be here? We're safe enough right now, but we can't stay here long. We have only a little water."

"We've got to take things as they come," said Jack grimly. "Right now we've got to save our lives."

The sun had come up and it promised to be a hot day, even if it was January. Since they were on the summit of the hill without any shade of any kind, they did not look forward to a very com-fortable day under the hot sun.

"Everything quiet on my side," said Jack.

"Here, too," said Bill.

"I do not see a sign of an Apache," said Little

Jim, who crawled from one side of the barrier to the other. "But I expect we will know very soon what they have planned for us. I do not trust the Apache."

"Neither do we," laughed Jack.

The Indians seemed to have entirely disappeared. The sun grew hotter. There was no wind and nothing stirred. Jack and Bill became restless.

"I think they have gone," said Jack finally. "I believe we should try to make the Cornudas station. Our water is gone, and I'm getting pretty thirsty."

"But we may find more Indians there," replied Bill. "That is a favorite watering place. Even if those we saw haven't returned to Cornudas, other Indians will probably be there. Anyway, I think this is a good time to strike out southwest over the plains, instead of sticking to the trail."

"Perhaps so, but what about water?"

"Well, we are bound to run across a band of antelope," continued Bill. "If we watch them closely and don't frighten them, sooner or later they'll lead us to some water."

"I would like to say something," said Little Jim. The others nodded. "It is that we do not see any antelope now. There are many antelope in these parts. When we passed here before there were many antelope. We can see for a long distance here, and we have not seen an antelope."

"Yes, that is true," said Jack. "But what is it you are trying to say?"

"Only that there are Apaches all around us," said Little Jim. "That is why there are no antelope."

"But how could there be Apaches around?" asked Bill. "It would be hard for them to hide."

"You do not know the Apache," continued Little Jim. "The Apache can hide on the open plain. He can become a tree. He can become a rock. He can become the grass itself. You will ride along, and the first thing you know an Apache jumps out before you."

The two men looked at each other.

"That's right," said Jack. "Yes, they are pretty clever in concealing themselves. Perhaps Jim here is right, and we should wait until darkness."

"But this heat! I'm being baked alive," said Bill.

Little Jim was looking over the rock barrier on the west side. "If you will look," he said softly, "you will see that the big round rock near the bottom of the hill is moving."

"Moving?" cried Jack. "What do you mean the rock is moving?"

Both men went to Little Jim's side and peered

cautiously over the rock barrier. "Well, it is moving!" exclaimed Bill.

"And look over there!" said Jack. "That one's moving, too."

"I can't believe it," said Bill, rubbing his eyes. "It must be the heat, or the heat waves." He looked again.

"There is an Apache behind each of those rocks," said Little Jim, bringing up his rifle. "I will soon have the chance to use the new rifle Don Jaime Gault gave to me."

"Well, I can't believe it—I mean about those Apaches pushing up those rocks," said Bill in wonder. "That is the smartest trick I've ever seen. They can get right up here without our getting a chance to shoot at them."

"It must take a lot of strength to push those rocks," said Jack. "However, the hill's not too steep, and the rocks are almost round. Look, there must be a dozen of those rocks moving now!"

Little Jim touched Jack's sleeve. "There are a lot of these round rocks up here, too," the boy said.

"Sure, there are lots of them. Oh, I see . . . I see," replied Jack. "You mean we could——"

"We could start some of them rolling down," said Little Jim, grinning.

"Well, it's worth a try," said Bill.

There were now a dozen rocks moving upward toward them inch by inch. They were being pushed so slowly and carefully that unless each one was watched closely it could hardly be seen to move.

"There is a rock right in front of us," said Little Jim, laying down his rifle. "It can be pushed right down on that other one."

Through a crack between two rocks of the barricade Jack could see the one Little Jim meant. "But you must be careful. They might take a shot at you," said Jack.

"I will crawl through between those rocks," Little Jim said. "The Apaches are downhill and cannot see me when I am close to the ground. I will start the rock down. When it hits the rock behind which there is an Apache, he will jump. Then you both shoot. Even if it does not hit his rock, when it passes by he will jump and will show some of himself. Then you can shoot."

"All right, but be careful."

Little Jim began to wriggle on his stomach through the space between the two rocks of the barricade. Jack and Bill watched him nervously, tensely holding their rifles in their hands. Little Jim moved until he was behind the round rock. Then he peeped from behind it at the one he hoped to hit. After this he turned around, lay on his back, placing his feet against the rock. He gave a push. The rock, which in time would have started downhill of its own accord, began to move. Little Jim flopped over on his stomach and quickly wriggled behind another rock near-by.

Jack and Bill watched the rock as it gained momentum. It bounced down the hill toward the rock one of the Apaches was pushing upward. Although for a moment it seemed as if it would smash into the Indian's rock, it just grazed it and rolled on. But its passing caused the Indian behind the rock to jerk himself to the side and expose his body.

The men fired their rifles as one. There was a yell, and they could see the Indian floundering behind the rock.

"Got him!" cried Jack.

"Looks like it," agreed Bill.

The Indian's rock rolled back a few feet, and then stopped. The rock Little Jim had pushed kept on rolling until it struck the trail, bounced over, and disappeared.

Another rock now started rolling downhill as the Indian behind it jumped up and rushed over to his fallen comrade.

"You take him, Jack," said Bill.

But before Jack could get his aim and pull the trigger there was a sharp crack. The Indian spun around, fell to the ground, and began to roll down the hill.

"I have tried out my new rifle and it works well," said Little Jim, lying beside the two men. "I shall tell Don Jaime Gault that it has done good work."

"That was good shooting with a twenty-two caliber," said Jack.

"It sure was," said Bill. "But get busy—look at those other Indians running downhill."

Sure enough, the Indians who had been engaged in edging rocks upward toward the fortress now abandoned them and fled. The rifles cracked; two Indians fell. The others dashed across the trail and down below to where the rest of their group was hiding.

"That takes care of them for a time," said Jack, mopping his face with a red bandanna. "What will they think of next?"

He had hardly spoken, before a score of Apaches appeared on the trail, waving their rifles and shouting. They started up the hill, apparently planning to take the barricade by assault.

"I'll take the ones on the left, you take those

on the right. Jim, you take the center ones," ordered Jack.

"No, I will watch the rear—it is a trick," said
Little Jim. He wriggled about and crawled to the
other side. He had hardly reached there before
he put his rifle to his shoulder, drew a bead on one
of two Indians crawling up the hill, and fired. The
Indian gave a yell, dropped his rifle, and fled, followed by his companion.

Jack and Bill were busy. But at their first volley
the Indians fell flat and began shooting. Bullets
whined, thudded against the rock barricade, and
kicked up the dust near-by.

"What were you shooting at?" asked Jack over
his shoulder.

"It was like I thought," called Little Jim. "Those
Apaches on your side were only trying to trick us.
Two were coming up from this side. But now they
have gone."

"These are crawling back, too," said Jack.

The fire from the Apaches stopped almost as
suddenly as it had begun. The Indians retreated
from the trail and disappeared once more.

"But what I can't understand," said Bill, "is how
those others managed to get across the trail and

up behind those rocks they were pushing. We were watching all the time."

"I will tell you, *señores*, how it happened," said Little Jim. "When we first got to this place and the Indians started shooting at us and we started shooting at them, you remember they all at once were gone. They hid themselves below the trail, down the hill. But before this, some of them left their horses and rolled into the dry grass beside the trail. The others took their horses away. Then, they crawled along until they got behind those rocks."

"And we didn't see them!" exclaimed Bill.

"No, if you look down now, you will see that you can only see the middle of the trail. The trail is worn down just enough so there is a place there where an Apache can keep from sight."

"Of course!" exclaimed Jack. "Just a couple of feet. I remember now. . . . There may be some behind that little bluff right now."

"Well, all we can do is to wait and see," grumbled Bill. "I'd like a drink of water, and am almost ready to make a dash for that spring at the Cornudas."

But they decided to wait until nightfall before leaving the trail and striking out through the plains and mountains for Ysleta. They lay in the hot sun throughout the afternoon without seeing any signs of the Apaches.

That night, before the moon rose, they silently left their barricade, crawled down the hill, and then started running as hard as they could in the direction of Ysleta.

10. Pancho's Day

PANCHO WAS still at his post the next day, watching and waiting. As dawn came he arose from his spot, looked about him, and then made his familiar tour of inspection, trotting around the adobe walls.

Finding nothing unusual, he trotted inside the enclosure and dragged out the antelope shoulder blade. Pancho settled down, the bone held between his paws, and began his breakfast.

When he had gnawed all the meat and gristle left on the bone, Pancho dug a hole and pushed the bone into it. He then covered it with the dirt he had taken from the hole, raking it in with one paw and then the other. Finally he smoothed the ground by shoveling the dirt with his nose. This done, he trotted away, his tail curled high, his mouth in a grin.

He went as usual to the entrance and with nose, ears, and eyes tried to learn if his masters and Little Jim were approaching. But he could smell nothing of them, nor hear any sound of footsteps. There was not even a cloud of dust in the distance that would have told him they were coming at last. He yawned and when he closed his mouth he let out a prolonged whine.

Pancho once more trotted around the adobe walls to see that everything was in order. He had made the circuit so often that he had already begun to wear a path around the walls.

In his path was a hill of red ants. Since Pancho's last round they had thrown up a little pile of earth around their newly formed hole. Pancho, his nose close to the ground, paused to observe these tiny creatures. Many were moving along in a double file, one line going toward the hole and the other from it. Several other ants were tugging at something about the size of one of Pancho's toes. He bent down closer to sniff this object, his nose al-

most touching it. Suddenly he felt a tickling sensa-
tion on the tip of his nose; an ant had crawled
upon it. Pancho quickly knocked the ant off with
his paw, sprang back, and barked.

The ants no longer interesting him, he stepped
gingerly over the ant hill and continued his round.
Two doves were cooing in the cedar tree near the
spring. A hawk was soaring back and forth, sweep-
ing along lazily on outspread wings, his head cocked
down in search of a rabbit or other small animal.
Higher up in the sky an eagle circled.

Just as certain creatures came forth at night in
search of prey and then disappeared when day
broke, now others came out of hiding to busy themselves in their quest for food or to bask in the sunshine. A horned toad, with sharp spines on his head,
a short thin tail, and scaly sides and back, ran out
of Pancho's path. He stopped on his short legs,
turned his head completely around as if on a
swivel, and stared with his beady little eyes at this
intruder. Pancho did not like this creature's looks.
He knew from experience that his spines and scales
were sharp. He decided to leave him alone and
made a circle around him. The toad's head swiveled
again, the better to follow Pancho's actions.

Pancho took several steps, then paused, his ears

pricked forward. What was that sound? Whatever it was must be just around the corner of the adobe wall. Pancho advanced warily. There was the sound again! There was no mistaking it now. It was a whirring sound—the sound of rattlers. A rattlesnake! Pancho now could smell the musty odor of the rattler.

Placing one foot carefully before the other, Pancho went to the corner and peered around. There was a sharp rustling sound. The rattlesnake was just around the corner, and with lightning-like rapidity it struck at Pancho's nose. Pancho jerked back just in time.

Pancho became more careful. He drew away from the wall and made a wider circuit. The rattlesnake, which had been drawn to the east side of the wall by the warmth of the morning sun, was coiled in the middle of Pancho's path. The rattler's head, broad and flat, with a forked tongue flicking back and forth from his mouth, was pointed toward Pancho. The snake's yellow eyes glistened. It was a large snake, about twice as long as Pancho's body and twice the size of his foreleg.

Ordinarily Pancho would have merely barked at the reptile, made several feints toward him in order to tease him and watch him strike out; but now Pancho felt differently. He would have to travel this path throughout the day, and he did not care to detour the snake each time. He would have to dispose of it once and for all.

Pancho, crouching close to the ground, advanced slowly, his muscles tightened like coiled springs, his neck extended. Inch by inch he moved. The snake's rattlers whirred their fearsome warning. The snake's head drew back, his forked tongue

flicking faster in and out of his mouth. This reptile could strike in one tenth of a second and within two thirds of its own length.

As Pancho edged nearer, the rustling sound of the rattlers became louder. The snake was ready to strike, to sink his ugly fangs into the head of his opponent. Pancho came closer.

Then the snake struck. Pancho jerked his head

to the side, leaping forward at the same time. The snake's fangs missed their mark, and before the snake could recoil, Pancho sank his teeth into its body, just behind its head. His teeth clenched. With a mighty effort he began to shake the snake. Its long body lashing Pancho's sides, he shook and shook it until he was sure there was no more fight in it. Then he released his hold and leaped back.

The snake was not dead yet. His body squirmed, and his rattlers whirred, but his head was a bloody, mangled mass. While he probably would not die until sundown, he was no longer a dangerous creature; he would strike no more. Pancho stepped amidst the squirming mass, and once more sinking his teeth into the snake's body, dragged it out of his path. He stood for a moment watching it, and then trotted away.

His victory over the snake made Pancho feel good. He held his head high, his mouth grinning, his tail curled. He got halfway round the adobe walls when he saw a flock of wild turkeys, led by an old tom turkey so large that he was half the size of Pancho. He was a lordly and saucy old bird, and when he saw Pancho he gobbled several times and stretched his neck as far as he could, holding his head very high. His hens, who were scattered about busily picking seeds and insects, seemed to pay little attention to their lord and master's call.

Having within him the instinct to herd, this was a challenge Pancho could not ignore. These hens should be bunched up, he seemed to decide, and the old tom should be taught a lesson.

As Pancho trotted in the direction of the flock of turkeys the old tom gave a loud warning, gobbling furiously. He stood his ground, and his feathers spread out angrily. Pancho went directly toward him. The tom cocked his head and glared at him, his wattles and comb becoming violently red. Pancho jumped forward, his forefeet slanting, his rump in the air, his tail waving from side to side.

Pancho barked; the tom spread his wings, lowered his head, and charged. Pancho leaped to the side and as the tom passed, Pancho snapped at his tail feathers. The tom wheeled and came at Pancho again. Once more Pancho leaped aside, barking excitedly, and this time he caught a tail feather in his teeth and pulled it out.

The turkey hens sent up a noisy clatter and ran together into a group. The tom charged again and again, and each time Pancho leaped from his path and snapped at him as he went by. The tom's charges were gradually becoming less violent. He was tiring and several of his tail feathers already were missing. Pancho was enjoying himself immensely. He was working this fighting old rascal as he wished, unafraid of the tom's beak or his spurs.

All at once the tom gave up. He raced over to where his hens were grouped, as if he suddenly realized they were unprotected. All fight was out of him. Pancho followed him closely. The turkeys, necks stretched and heads high, eyed him in fright. Pancho circled them and closed them into a more compact mass. Then he began to drive them toward the stage station. He raced from side to side, barking and snapping at the confused birds. He drove them through the entrance and placed himself on guard there to see that they did not get out. The turkey hens huddled in one corner, too frightened to utter a sound. The old tom, however, continued to gobble angrily.

Pancho soon tired of this game. He sat on his haunches, his great tongue lolling from the side of his mouth. As he looked down the trail his thoughts were once more on Jack and Bill and Little Jim. They had been gone a long time.

Feeling thirsty after so much effort, Pancho

trotted over to the spring. Some small birds that had been fluttering in the water at the edge, flew up and lighted in the cedar tree. Pancho lapped up several tonguesful of water. He heard something behind him, and looking around, saw the turkeys coming out of the stage station. He raced back and drove them inside.

He sat down once more, and finally lay down and stretched out his paws. The sun was nice and warm. His head sank down, and his jowl rested on his forefeet. He snapped lazily at a fly. Finally his eyes closed. For a time his ears flicked back and forth, then were still. Pancho was tired and he sank into a light sleep.

Pancho felt something touch him. As if a spring had been suddenly released inside him, he shot into the air and came down on all fours—his back bristled, his tail spread out, his teeth bared.

There in front of him was a ridiculous little creature. It drew back when Pancho leaped up, stood a moment, then gave a grunt and came toward him. Pancho growled and stepped back. The piglike little fellow, still grunting, continued to advance. It seemed to want to make friends.

Pancho backed and side-stepped to be in a better position to attack. But something told him the small creature did not want to fight. He was a collared peccary, with a white band around his neck, bristly and with grizzled gray-black hair. His round, flat snout worked up and down as he sniffed. His piggish little eyes danced merrily. He was not yet full-grown.

Pancho, edging back as the peccary came on, finally raced around him and barked. The peccary turned in his tracks and watched Pancho. He kept grunting in a friendly fashion. Pancho let his fore-legs slide forward, his rump up, his tail wagging. He barked several times and again raced around the peccary to try to obtain a better scent of him without getting in the way of his small white tusks.

Finally, Pancho sank on his haunches and waited. The peccary came toward him without fear. Pancho let him get directly in front of him and then leaped over his back, raced around him, and barked. The peccary would not let Pancho get behind him, but kept turning. He did not appear frightened, but continued to grunt.

Pancho approached the peccary warily. This time the little creature did not move, but kept sniffing with his round, flat nose. Pancho started to touch noses, thought better of it and leaped back, barking, his tail wagging. The peccary seemed surprised. Pancho advanced again. This time they touched noses. The peccary gave a satisfied grunt; Pancho barked. The peccary trotted toward the spring, and Pancho followed. The little animal settled in the mud, grunting contentedly, and then lay down and wallowed. Pancho, who watched all this, barked again. The peccary, after completely covering himself with mud, finally came out.

Pancho now heard a very loud, deep grunt. Wheeling, he saw a larger peccary a few yards away. It had long sharp tusks, and its eyes glared at Pancho in an unfriendly way. This one was not to be trifled with. Pancho growled and his neck hair rose. Well, a fight was a fight. He was ready.

But nothing like that happened. The smaller peccary trotted up to the older one, touched snouts, grunted, and rubbed against the other. The older one seemed to be saying "Come on, you've had enough of this creature. He's not one for you to play with." The two started off. After a few steps, the smaller peccary stopped, turned, and looked toward Pancho. Pancho wagged his tail and barked; the peccary grunted. Then the two peccaries trotted away.

Pancho looked after them. Then he sighed and sank to the ground. Behind him, the turkey tom gobbled. Once more the tom had got up his courage and started to lead his hens out of the station. Pancho arose and gave a warning bark. The turkey tom and hens turned and went back.

As the day wore on, Pancho made several trips to see what the red ants were doing. He also took a look at the rattler. Its tail was still twitching; it seemed to die gradually from head to tail. Pancho gazed into the distance to see if the small peccary were around. Then he investigated the ambulance, rising on his hind legs to look in the rear. As he did so something next to him appeared to move. He leaped back to the ground, growling, with his teeth bared.

He stood a moment, and hearing nothing, he cautiously rose to look inside the ambulance again. He suddenly was confronted with the face of a dog. He leaped back once more, this time barking loudly. He sniffed and sniffed. He could smell no dog. He listened carefully. He could hear nothing that sounded like a dog.

Once more he placed his forepaws on the tail-gate, his neck hairs standing up, deep growls coming from his throat. He looked, and the dog looked back at him. Pancho drew back slightly, sniffing, and then growling. He became bolder. As he pushed his nose toward the other dog, that dog seemed to push his nose closer to Pancho's. He saw the dog's eyes glaring directly into his own eyes. But still no smell! Something must be wrong.

Pancho's nose finally touched a cool, smooth surface. His nose pressed against the other dog's. No smell. Pancho was puzzled, and he barked. He dropped to the ground and continued to bark. Then he rose again and looked at the other dog, reflected in a shaving mirror which hung just inside the ambulance. The dog looked back at him, but Pancho could get no scent of him. He moved all right, but it was the scent that mattered to Pancho.

Pancho touched noses again. This meant nothing. He stood a moment glaring into the eyes of his image, growling in a puzzled way. He sniffed and sniffed. Well, he would ignore this other dog. A dog without a scent was certainly not worth bothering about.

Pancho sniffed at his bacon. He turned quickly and saw the dog in the mirror looking directly into his eyes. He dragged the hunk of bacon out of the ambulance, pulling it underneath on the sacks. He sank down, and holding the bacon between his paws, tore off several bites. He swallowed without chewing. The salt meat made him thirsty, so he again trotted to the spring and took a drink. Then he returned and once more rose and looked at his image. He let himself down, glanced at the turkeys to see that they were safe, and then went to the entrance. He settled down in the afternoon sun.

The landscape shimmered under the hot sun. In the distance he could see a band of antelope. They seemed never to be still, always taking fright at something. Each time there would be a flash of white as their signal hairs spread out, and they would dash away. The hawk continued to soar back and forth.

Night came and Pancho again made his rounds of the stage station. Then he came back to the entrance, where he lay down with his nose toward the trail, his ears pricked for any welcome sound. The turkeys gobbled softly as they roosted on the wheels of the ambulance. They could leave if they wished. Pancho did not care.

The three-quarters moon rose, spreading its silver light over the landscape. A wolf howled in the distance. Pancho lifted his head from his paws and whined. The wolf howled again. Pancho's hair rose on his neck, and he growled. He tried to get a whiff of the wolf, but he could smell nothing.

Soon another wolf answered. In time there was

a chorus of howls. The sounds floated through the night air and seemed to linger there. Pancho ceased growling. He lay still and listened. Some mysterious inner force made him want to howl in answer. Several times he raised his head, his mouth forming in an O-shape, but no sound came. He yawned instead, dropped his jowl on his paws, and watched down the trail.

11. The Call of the Wolf

As the days passed, Pancho settled into a routine. He roamed the stage station at night, making his usual tour around the adobe walls, where he had worn a path. He jealously guarded the spring, making sure that only those animals which he approved drank there. He slept but little.

He certainly would not sleep on a moonlight night, because as long as he had been with human beings—and that, of course, had been all his life —he knew that they were always on the alert when the moon was full. He did not know that it was then they feared an Apache raid, for Indians never attacked in darkness. They came in full daylight, or in the very early dawn, or on moonlight nights. White men called a full moon an Apache Moon, and they prepared for danger. They believed, perhaps without reason, that Indians thought they went to the happy hunting grounds under the same conditions that they died. If they died in darkness, their spirits would be forced to wander ever after in darkness. They took no chances.

Pancho knew nothing about this. He only knew that on such nights the men were nervous and worried and always posted guards. He felt this nervousness, and he kept awake then; he helped to guard.

Daytime was not so bad. It was then that Pancho obtained his half sleep. The north wind still blew, but it came across sun-heated plains. Pancho had nothing to do but wait. He had lost interest in the flock of turkeys and had watched them indifferently as they filed out of the stage station the morning after he had imprisoned them.

The dead rattlesnake had become a bad odor for a time as beetles and ants and worms began to consume its body. Pancho had angrily killed a large tarantula by bringing his paw down on the ugly creature. He had not studied it, walked around

it, teased it, or sought to make it mad. He had just
killed it and walked on. A whip scorpion scurried
across his path and left behind a smell of vinegar
—which caused some to call these creatures vine-
garroons—and Pancho passed on, merely sneezing
to free his nostrils of the sharp odor. He had even
lost interest in the dog-face in the mirror and
rarely gazed at it.

The little peccary, which might have made an
interesting playmate, had not come back. Possibly its mother had scolded it and taken it far
away. Anyway, Pancho did not feel like romping
and playing, chasing birds, or barking at horned
toads. He was just staying there as he had been
ordered. He could not reason why he was to stay,
or how long he was to stay; he had simply been
told "Don Francisco, you stay here!"

So he curled in the sun at the entrance of the
station, his nose pointed toward the trail over
which Jack and Bill and Little Jim had gone, and
waited. He would sometimes twitch in his dreams,
and growl softly. Then he would wake with a jerk,
prick his ears, and look about him. After such in-
terruptions of his sleep he would yawn, start to lay
his head on his flank, think better of it, and get
up. He would yawn again, and then trot about

the adobe walls, sniffing here and there, to see that
the remains of his bacon were safe. Finally, he
would return to his post at the entrance.

The moon came up as usual. This night it was
a full moon. With its rising came the cries of
wolves and coyotes. Pancho welcomed the sound.
He no longer growled. The hair of his neck no
longer bristled. He listened to the yelps of coyotes
and the baying of the wolves and seemed to know
that these voices were not raised in warning cries,
or frightened cries, or hunting cries. These were
sad cries, a sort of plaintive calling to each other
or to the moon-spirit above. It was a lonesome
sound and Pancho was lonesome. He had a desire
to answer these voices. . . .

Wolves were Pancho's enemies, but his ancestors
had been wolves. Not the lean gray wolves of the
Texas plains and mountains, but those of the mountains and valleys of a faraway land. Some instinct
deep inside him stirred, made him want to return
to the wild, carefree life of his ancestors. But
Pancho was also a tame animal who had been
taught a sense of duty. This sense of duty was a
leash which held him back. He had been born
with the instincts of the wolf, but like his father
and his father's father before him, he had been

taught to obey the words of man. Obedience was second nature. Loyalty and obedience. He had always been called on daily to show this loyalty and to do as he was told. But it had been days now since he had heard anyone say "Down, Pancho!" or "Go get that, Pancho!" or "Don Francisco, you stay here!"

The wolves were howling in a regular chorus now. Their cries seemed to fill the air. Pancho got up on his four legs. He jerked his head up and down as he sniffed the air, but he could detect no disturbing scent.

The wolves continued to bay. The sound of their voices seemed to come in waves, in a kind of rhythm. It was a stronger, more commanding force than the memory of Little Jim's words of command, the sense of obedience and loyalty he had learned from the time he was born. All these seemed to fade away.

He threw back his head, his noise pointing upward, and gave a deep, resounding howl, one that filled the night air and drowned out the cries of the wolves. In this melancholy call Pancho seemed to voice all his longing to join the wolf pack, tear at the throat of the leader, and trot triumphantly off at the head of his kinsmen of the plains and mountains.

As his call died away there was a sudden silence. The other wolves stopped their baying at once, as if from fright or in admiration. But there was no mistaking the effect his own act had on Pancho. Hardly had the last note of his call faded away than Pancho seemed to realize that he had done something wrong. He glanced about quickly, as if he expected to see Little Jim with a surprised look on his face, or Jack or Bill looking at him accusingly. He dropped his tail between his legs and slunk off.

He might have gone and curled beneath the ambulance and remained there until he felt his act had been forgotten, but there came a soft sound to his ears, and his nose picked up the unmistakable scent of wolf. Pancho wheeled about. His forelegs spread, his tail bushed, his neck and back hairs bristled, his lips curled back from his teeth; he was all at once full of fight. A wolf in the distance baying at the moon was one thing, but a wolf approaching stealthily to invade Pancho's territory was another.

Then in the full moonlight he saw the invader. The animal seemed unafraid and was trotting toward Pancho. He was a large gray wolf, as big as Pancho, but fiercer looking, with a heavier underjaw. In the moonlight he looked almost white.

While wolves had howled all about Pancho for nights, none had dared approach the stage station. Why this one came now was a mystery. Having heard Pancho's howl, he might have thought he was another wolf, and he had come to join him. Or he might have considered the call a challenge to him. He was probably the leader of the wolf pack. It was hard to tell whether he came as a friend or an enemy.

Pancho crouched close to the ground and waited. The wolf slowed down to a walk and then stopped. He sniffed the air, but since he was coming with the wind, he could smell nothing. Pancho waited, close to the ground, his muscles tense, his tail barely moving from side to side. There was a sort of gurgle in his throat as he growled. The wolf heard the low growl; his ears pointed forward, and his eyes gleamed. While most wolves are cowards, especially when alone, and will only attack and fight in packs, this one was unafraid. He had come for some purpose, and whatever it was, he was going to see it through. He advanced a step.

This was enough for Pancho. With a snarl he leaped forward and in two bounds was in front of the wolf. The other bristled, showed his fangs, and snarled his anger. Pancho leaped to his right to attack the wolf from the side, but the wolf quickly turned. Pancho tried to circle him, but the wolf was too quick.

Suddenly the wolf sprang at Pancho, who flung himself out of the way. The wolf hurtled past, and as he went by, Pancho leaped in and sank his teeth into the wolf's shoulder. The two went over and over on the ground, growling fiercely. The wolf's teeth snapped angrily. He twisted about, with Pancho still hanging on by his teeth, and snapped at Pancho's foreleg. Pancho released his hold when he felt the wolf's teeth close on his leg, and caught the wolf's ear in his teeth. The wolf yelped and let go. The two backed off from each other.

The wolf looked about him as if expecting help. Pancho looked too, and he saw a half circle of gleaming eyes and open red mouths. The wolf pack had closed in.

Pancho snarled at the wolves around him. He backed up a little toward the stage station, where he felt more secure, but the wolf sprang at him again. They rolled over and over on the ground, snapping at each other, but neither was able to fasten on. The wolf was trying for Pancho's throat, and his teeth clicked together loudly when he missed.

Once more the two were on their feet and began

to circle each other. From the terrific fight they had just had it was likely that one or both would be bitten and clawed until he could not get up. The wolf showed signs of injury. His left ear was bloody and torn. Pancho's leg was bleeding.

Pancho made a feint to leap in. The wolf twisted to meet his attack, but Pancho darted to the other side, lowered his head, and caught the wolf by

the throat. The wolf squirmed and fought, but Pancho held on. The wolf rolled on his back, his claws tearing into Pancho's flesh, but he did not release his hold. Pancho sunk his teeth deeper. Then he began to shake his antagonist. The wolf's efforts became weaker and weaker, and soon he lay still. Pancho held on firmly and continued to shake him.

Finally Pancho tried to let go. It was difficult, for he had locked his teeth in the wolf's throat, and at first he could not open his jaws. Then, with an effort, he opened them. The wolf did not move. Pancho tasted the wolf's blood, and it angered him even more. He seemed to remember the half circle of wolves about him that had begun to draw back when they saw their leader getting the worst of it. Had the wolf gotten the better of Pancho, they would have rushed in. Now they only waited to see what Pancho would do. He had whipped the leader. Would he now lead the pack? When he showed his intentions, the other wolves would rush in and tear the fallen leader to pieces.

But Pancho would have nothing of this. He faced the pack defiantly, ready for one or all of them to start forward, if they dared. He would fight them singly or all at once. His feet spread, his tail waving, his blood-covered mouth grinning, he challenged them all.

The wolves appeared puzzled. Finally they began to slink back and were soon gone. In the distance other wolves howled, and soon these wolves would be howling, too. Pancho stood guard over the fallen wolf. He expected him to rise and resume the fight, but the wolf would fight no more.

Pancho began to lick his own wounds. His leg was very painful, for the wolf's teeth had sunk deeply in it; his belly and parts of his face had been cut by the wolf's claws.

Pancho sank down beside the dead wolf. After he had taken care of his own wounds, he lay there for a time, listening to the night sounds. Now and then he turned his head toward the trail.

12. The Apache Visitor

PANCHO'S MEAT WAS GONE. He stood up on his hind legs and clawed open the sack of corn in the rear of the ambulance. As the grain came out, Pancho began to eat it. He chewed and chewed, the kernels crackling between his teeth. He was unaccustomed to working so hard to get food. Normally, he rarely chewed anything; he simply gulped it down. But these small kernels had to be chewed, and Pancho was so hungry that they tasted good.

When he had eaten enough of the corn, he dropped back to the ground on all fours. But he quickly lifted his right forefoot because of the pain. The leg was swollen, and the wound made by the wolf's teeth was still open and bleeding. Pancho lay down and licked the wound.

After a while, he felt thirsty. He hopped on three legs to the spring, where he lapped up some water. He started to leave, but his mouth was hot and dry, so he turned back and lapped up some more. Then he hopped over to the entrance of the stage station and lay down in his accustomed spot. It was daylight now, and he could see the trail. He watched it for a time, but as usual he saw no one coming along it. Although he had no way of knowing it, it had been ten days since his masters left. And during that time Pancho had watched the trail almost continuously.

Several large black birds circled in the air above him. Having spotted the body of the wolf, they were anxious to feast on it. Pancho watched them, growling softly to himself. He knew what they wanted.

The buzzards circled lower, making strange sounds. One of them lighted on the ground several feet away from the wolf's body. He began to stride toward it, his neck extended. Pancho got to his feet and hopped over to the wolf's body.

The large bird backed away and then took flight, giving a disappointing squawk.

Pancho sniffed the dead wolf, whose odor seemed stronger than ever. He bristled in spite of himself. Sniffing the wolf once more, he hopped back to his post at the entrance. The buzzards continued to circle. Pancho growled.

These birds were looking forward to a feast. They were not going to give up so easily. Pancho knew what they expected. He felt hungry, too, for the corn had not satisfied him. A big, healthy dog like him needed meat. He licked his chops, whined a little, and then let his jowl fall on his forefeet.

After a while, an antelope, shy and ready to dart away at the slightest indication of danger, came into sight a hundred yards or so from him. Pancho waited for it to come nearer. This was what he wanted. The antelope was meat he could eat. He raised his head slightly and licked his chops.

But the antelope did not come nearer. The breeze had died down, so it couldn't have got any warning scent from Pancho's direction; yet something kept it from coming toward the stage station. Pancho watched the animal moving farther and farther away in its search for grass. He became restless; he would have to go after the antelope.

Pancho got to his feet. His leg hurt, but it did not matter. He had to have food. He started toward the antelope, his belly close to the ground.

Pancho had gone only a short distance when he stopped. He was leaving his post. The antelope might take him on a long chase, and the post would be unprotected. He had been told to stay there. He had to stay. He turned about and went back, occasionally turning to look forlornly at the antelope.

Conscious of his hurt leg again, he hopped toward the ambulance and rose on his hind feet to eat more corn. After another visit to the spring he took up his post at the entrance.

Pancho, his head between his forepaws, crouched low beside the adobe wall of the state station and watched the approach of a horseman. This horseman was an Indian, an Apache. He was riding up to the stage station with the wind, and Pancho had scented him even before he came into sight.

Usually Pancho would have gone to meet this enemy halfway, for the smell and sight of an Apache caused him to lose all sense of his own safety. His impulse was to attack, and to attack at once.

Now, however, he seemed to know that he

would need all his strength to overcome his foe. He could not afford to waste his energy by forcing the fight. He was weak from lack of the proper food, and his leg was almost useless from the wolf bite. He must wait until his enemy was close and then spring, summoning all his strength to the best advantage.

During the days that had passed since his fight with the wolf, a change had come over Pancho. He seemed more like the savage, wild creatures about him. Wild animals, knowing by instinct that each battle is a fight to the death, stalk their enemies, watching warily for some moment when they are off guard, or quietly awaiting their approach to surprise them and pounce on them. Had the little piglike animal come back now, Pancho would not have been curious about him. He would not have romped about and tried to play with him. No, he would have leaped on him, torn him to pieces, and then sunk down to eat his kill, tugging at the flesh and growling to himself.

He was hungry, almost starved. The corn had not satisfied his hunger. His insides were empty and complaining. He had never known hunger like this. But still he did not desert his post, dash out over the plains looking for something to kill and eat. Something still kept him to his duty. It was as if he knew nothing else. He had been told to stay, and he had understood. He would stay.

The horseman approached carefully. Every so often he reined in his pony, then shielded his eyes with his hand and peered toward the stage station. The dummies rigged up on the wall did not receive his attention. He probably now realized they were not men. He was looking for something else —something that moved.

But nothing moved. Several small birds were flitting about the stage station walls, now disappearing as they flew down inside, and then flying up. Some even lighted on the walls. There was certainly nothing there if these birds were not frightened. This must have been what the Apache warrior thought, for he now rode toward the station confidently.

Pancho watched him. As he came nearer, Pancho crouched closer to the wall behind some wild-grape vines which sheltered it.

A fly lighted on Pancho's nose. Still he did not move. He hated flies and always snapped at them. Sometimes he got them, too. They were bothersome creatures and bit his ears. Once the blood started to flow, others came and soon there were great sores on his ears.

He looked down his nose at the fly, his eyes

crossing in the effort to focus them. The fly did not
move. It arched its back, and its stinger shot out
and into Pancho's nose. He growled. The fly had
its stinger firmly in the skin and was pumping
away. It paid no attention to the growl. The little
needle hurt Pancho, but still he did not move.

The brave's pinto pony was now a few yards
from the wall and Pancho watched him through
the vines. The Apache's eyes sparkled with greed,
for he could see many shiny things in the ambulance. He urged his pony a few steps closer and
started to dismount.

Suddenly, a long back figure shot through the
air. Pancho, leaping from a crouching position,
sprang directly at the rider. The pony gave a
frightened cry and reared. The Indian, almost
thrown from his back, hung onto the pony's mane.
The pony reared on its hind legs and pawed the
air. The rider was thrown off. Pancho missed him.

The Indian was on his feet when Pancho hit
the ground. Pancho wheeled, bared his teeth, and
crouched to spring again. The Indian raced for a
cedar tree near-by, grabbed a low branch, and
hoisted himself up. Pancho, leaping once more,
threw up his head as he passed beneath the man
and caught hold of his long breechcloth. The

breechcloth came off in Pancho's teeth. The Indian, clinging to the lower branch of the tree,
quickly pulled himself up higher.

Pancho shook the breechcloth angrily and then,
holding it with his paws, tore it into shreds. The
Indian, sitting in the tree, clad only in his leg-
gings and moccasins, watched the dog helplessly.
His rifle and the bow and arrows he carried had
been knocked to the ground when he was thrown
off the pony. His knife sheath and knife had been
jerked off when Pancho tore the breechcloth from
the warrior's belt.

The pony stopped a short distance away. He
was over his first fright and now was looking at
Pancho and his former rider with curiosity. Pancho
dashed after the pony, nipped at his heels, and
drove him into the stage station.

When Pancho left the tree the Apache made
a gesture as if he intended to get down and run.
Then, evidently realizing that he had no chance
of getting away on foot, he settled back on his
limb and watched.

Pancho came back to the tree. He reared on his
hind legs and reached as high as he could with
his forepaws, trying to get at the Indian. Then,
unmindful of his wounded leg, he came down on

four feet and circled the tree, looking up all the
time and whining.

The Indian's quirt lay on the ground where it
had fallen. Pancho sniffed it and the hair rose on
his neck. He recognized it at once. That quirt had
been used to strike him the night in Ysleta when
he and Little Jim had run into Jack One Day.
Pancho never forgot a smell. He took the quirt
between his teeth and shook it with all his might.
He held it down with his forepaws and pulled and
tugged at it with his teeth, tearing the rawhide
braid. It was as if he wanted to vent his wrath
on everything belonging to that Apache. Finally
he lay down with the quirt between his paws and
chewed on the leather lash. This was at least
something that could be eaten, and Pancho was
hungry.

The Apache sat on the tree limb, watching
Pancho with no expression on his bronzed face.
There was nothing for him to do but sit there and
wait. Wait for what? He did not know. But he
would watch and wait, and at the first opportunity
he would try to make his escape. He believed that
the two miners and the Pueblo boy must be near.
They would not go off and leave this dog alone.
The men's horses were gone, but they would re-

turn and rescue him from the dog. He was not anxious to fall into the hands of these white men, however, for they would give him over to the Rangers. Or perhaps they did not know he had stolen three horses from the Rangers. He would wait and see.

Meantime, he did not want to excite the dog further. At first, he had thought of breaking off a limb to throw at the dog, but if he missed, he would only make the dog more angry.

He now decided to speak softly to Pancho. "Good dog . . . good dog," he began.

At his first words Pancho arose to his feet and growled.

Perhaps the best thing to do would be to remain quiet and wait.

Pancho would wait, too. He would wait until that Apache came down. He would never leave until he got hold of that Apache. Nothing else mattered. His leg no longer hurt him.

13. The Rescue

"THERE IT IS," cried Little Jim. He pointed toward the old stage station at Crow Flat, a mile or so away. Then, as if ashamed of himself for showing his eagerness to see Pancho, he let his hand fall and said in a lower voice, "It looks just the way we left it twelve days ago. I guess Don Francisco is still watching things."

But Jim Gault, who was riding beside Little Jim, did not try to conceal his excitement. "Rattle-snakes and tarantulas!" he shouted. "There she is, boys. Let's get movin'." He loosened the reins and leaned forward, at the same time nudging his pony in the flanks with his heels.

"Whoopee!" came from behind him. Then the clear, stern voice of Lieutenant Baylor.

"Not so fast, boys." Jim Gault and the others slowed up. Lieutenant Baylor continued, "We'd better approach that place carefully. We've seen plenty of Indian signs along here. We don't want to walk into a trap. There may be a dozen or more Indians hiding inside those walls."

"You're right, Lieutenant," said Jim Gault. "It does appear sort of quietlike there. If that dog was still there, he'd be out a-barkin' and carrying on by this time. Guess we'd better approach on our bellies."

They slowed to a walk, and Little Jim, shading his eyes, looked toward the adobe walls. He could see nothing of Pancho. Then he thought he saw something in the cedar tree near the entrance. He squinted his eyes and peered at it intently. He was sure there was a man in that tree! An Indian!

"Look," he said to Lieutenant Baylor. "In that tree. There's an Indian up in that tree."

Lieutenant Baylor looked where Little Jim pointed. "I do believe there is a man there," he said.

"I see him!" exclaimed Jim Gault. "You were

right, Lieutenant. There're Indians there. They're waitin' for us for sure." He brushed his hat back and wiped his brow. "And me wanting to dash up there! You're plumb right."

"The Indian sees us," said Little Jim. "I believe he's signaling."

"Looks like he's waving to us," said Jim Gault.

They rode closer, carbines out of their scabbards, ready for action. "I can pick him off from here," said Jim Gault, bringing up his carbine.

"Wait a minute!" ordered Lieutenant Baylor. "There's something funny here. That Indian is signaling to us. He's trying to make us understand something. I can't figure this out."

"Well, we'd better watch out. I don't trust a redskin," grunted Jim Gault, lowering his carbine. He glanced at Little Jim, swallowed, and corrected himself. "An Apache, that is."

"He's an Apache, all right," said Little Jim. "I can tell by that yellow band around his head. He's an Apache, all right—but he seems to be in trouble. Something must be keeping him up that tree." Then Little Jim exclaimed, "Don Francisco! Don Francisco has him up that tree. I know it must be Don Francisco."

He started to urge his pony ahead. But Lieutenant Baylor stopped him. "Easy now, Jim," he said. "Let's not rush into this. It may be a trick of some kind. Anyway, I don't see your Don Francisco."

They could now see the Indian clearly, standing up on a branch, waving his arms. But they could not understand what he was trying to signal, nor could they see any sign of Pancho.

But Pancho was there, at the foot of the tree. He lay with his head turned up, watching the Indian. He had watched him all the day before and all through the night. He was hungry and thirsty, but he had not left his place for an instant, even though it was but a short distance to the spring. Foam flecked from his mouth; his eyes were bloodshot; his leg was swollen and sore; his ears were bleeding from fly bites. When he got up to change his position he staggered a little.

But when he looked up at his enemy he stiffened. All his strength would return if the Indian tried to get down that tree. He would tear him to pieces. Not a sound came from the dog, not a whimper. He just waited.

The Indian, forgetting his first decision, had broken off some tree branches and hurled them at Pancho. He had yelled at Pancho. He had tried talking softly, hoping to make friends. He had raved at him, he had spit at him, until now his mouth was so dry he could spit no more. Finally, he had chewed twigs to try to satisfy his thirst. Once or twice he had started down the tree just to see what the dog would do. Each time Pancho rose to his feet, bared his teeth, and waited. The Indian went back to his perch.

It hurt his pride to think of being held there by a dog. He wanted to be rescued, but certainly not by his own people. How would he ever live it down? Run up a tree and kept prisoner there by a dog! He would be the laughing stock of his entire tribe. When he had such thoughts he gritted his teeth and started down the tree. He would strangle that dog with his bare hands. But halfway down he looked into those bloodshot eyes and saw those fierce white teeth and changed his mind.

At last, the Indian saw horsemen approaching. There were too many of them to be the men who owned the ambulance. He could not tell from the distance whether they were white men or Indians. If they were white men, he was in for a bad time. If they were Indians, he would be saved, but he would have to face the jeers of his own kind.

Finally the horsemen were close enough for him

to see that they were white men, and soon he was certain they were Rangers as well. Texas Rangers! From Ysleta! Yes, that was Lieutenant Baylor's horse. The Indian recognized it immediately—that black horse with the white face and white feet. He knew that horse well. He had hoped to get away with it when he left with the other horses.

Well, he could explain why he had left. The horses he was watching had bolted, and he had chased them. He never did catch up with them. They had led him on and on, and he did not dare come back to the Ranger camp without the ponies. That is what he would tell them, Jack One Day said to himself, and he began to signal to the Rangers. He wanted them to hurry and call off this dog. He was ashamed of his predicament, but when a man needs a drink and something to eat, that comes first. Jack One Day wanted water and he wanted food.

When the Apache stood up in the tree and began to signal, Pancho also arose to his feet and growled. This was the first sound he had made in hours. Foam flecked from his mouth, and when Jack One Day looked down he was sure the dog was mad.

Pancho was too intent watching his enemy to notice the approach of the Rangers and Little Jim. The scent might have come to him, but he did not notice it. His senses were no longer keen; and if he saw dust arising from the horses' hoofs, or heard any sound, he paid no attention. He only watched the Indian, and then seeing him suddenly become active, he growled his hatred.

Twenty-five yards or more from the station Lieutenant Baylor held up his hand, signaling his men to halt. And it was only then that Little Jim, reining in his pony, saw Pancho. He could hardly believe his eyes. Pancho looked thin and gaunt and dirty. His hair was matted, his mouth was open, and his tongue hung out, swollen and red.

"Don Francisco!" called Little Jim.

Pancho did not hear, or if he did, he ignored the call. He was watching Jack One Day, and he never took his eyes from him. Nor did his ears prick up at the sound of Little Jim's voice.

"Why, that's Jack One Day in the tree!" exclaimed Lieutenant Baylor.

"Sure, that's the same varmint that ran off with my hoss!" cried Jim Gault. He raised his carbine, but Lieutenant Baylor held up his hand.

"Easy, Jim," he cautioned him.

Jack One Day in the tree, minus his breech-cloth, his dark eyes glittering in their sunken sockets, tried to say something. His lips moved, but no sound came.

"Call off that dog," said Lieutenant Baylor. "Let's get this Indian down. He's got a lot of explaining to do."

Little Jim had already dismounted. He walked toward Pancho. "Don Francisco . . . Don Francisco," he called softly, holding out his hand.

The dog still did not notice him. He stood, his legs widespread, his head slightly cocked to the side, watching Jack One Day.

"Watch out, son," called Lieutenant Baylor. "That dog is mad. He's gone mad."

Little Jim did not hear. He approached closer to Pancho, snapping his fingers, talking to him. "Don Francisco, it is I . . . Little Jim. Don Francisco . . . Don Francisco—" Little Jim was the length of his own body from the dog when, suddenly, Pancho saw him. He jumped back, growled, and showed his teeth.

"Don't go any nearer!" shouted Lieutenant Baylor. "Come back here. . . . That dog doesn't know you—he'll kill you."

Little Jim did not hesitate. Pancho was his friend.

Pancho would not bite him. He held out both hands. "Don Francisco . . . Don Francisco," he said.

"Watch out!" called Lieutenant Baylor. "I'm going to kill that dog. He's dangerous . . . he doesn't know you."

Lieutenant Baylor raised his carbine.

Pancho growled louder and gathered himself to spring. His ears were flat; the hair on his neck and back stood up straight.

Little Jim stepped directly in front of him.

Lieutenant Baylor's finger was on the trigger, but he could not shoot. Little Jim had kneeled in front of Pancho and caught the dog's head in his hands. Pancho's growls became whimpers, and Little Jim hugged him.

Suddenly the dog whined, broke away from Little Jim and raced around him, barking happily.

14. Pancho Joins the Rangers

"Now, don't go very far away. We will be leaving here in a short time," Jack Andrews called, as Little Jim walked away with Pancho.

Little Jim was going to San Antonio with Jack Andrews and Bill Wiswald. Pancho was to remain behind for a while. He had work to do. He had been assigned to Company C, Frontier Battalion, Texas Rangers under Lieutenant Baylor.

Little Jim wanted to explain this to his friend, and so the two walked through the narrow street of Ysleta down toward the river bank. When they got there Little Jim patted Pancho's back, and the dog lay down. Little Jim sat beside him, rested Pancho's head in his lap, and put his own head down so that it touched the dog's. Pancho's tail thumped the ground, and he whined contentedly.

"We must have a little talk, you and I, my friend," said Little Jim.

Pancho whined again and sought to lick Little Jim's face.

"I must explain to you why I am going away and you are staying here. You do not mind staying here a little while?"

Pancho whimpered in reply.

"It is good. It will not be for long. I am going to San Antonio, where I will enter school. Don Juan and Don Guillermo are kind. They will put me in school and provide for me."

Pancho thumped his tail.

"But you have been taken into the Texas Rangers as a scout, so you have work to do. They have a report that some of Victorio's band of Apaches are hidden in the Sierra Diablo Mountains here in Texas. The Rangers will go after them and will round them up and put them on a reservation. It may even be more serious than that. I do not believe they will ever take these Apaches alive.

But the Rangers will put an end to the trouble. You are glad to help round up the Apaches?"

Pancho growled at the word, but he whined again in answer. Little Jim understood.

"The Rangers know that you will quickly find the trail of the Apaches and will lead the way to them. That will be your job. After this is all over they will return to San Antonio and they will bring you with them. Then I shall see you once more, Don Francisco. We will both be happy." Little Jim paused. "Oh, there is something else," he said, taking some gold from a pouch hanging from his belt. "I have here thirty dollars from Don Jaime Gault. It is the reward he has paid you for getting back his pony, Glass Eye. You know that Glass Eye was the pony Jack One Day was riding when you ran him up that tree. You held the pony in the stage station, and Don Jaime Gault has paid me the money for you. He says you must have the best and biggest bones one can buy in San Antonio. You like that?"

Yes, Pancho liked that. He liked everything Little Jim said or did. He got to his feet, barked happily, and raced around Little Jim. He was happy and he wanted to play. He dashed toward the river, stopping to indicate that he wished Little Jim to throw something in the water so he could bring it out.

"No, we have no time now for play," replied Little Jim, getting up. "I will be leaving shortly, and I wish you to remain here like a good dog. Anyway, you cannot play with such a bad leg. Come here!"

Pancho, surprised at the tone in Little Jim's voice, lowered his tail and half slunk toward the boy.

"No, no, I am not scolding you," said Little Jim soothingly, rubbing Pancho's ears. "It is that I am asking you to remain here and do your work. Then we shall be together once more."

Pancho barked.

"You understand, Don Francisco?" said Little Jim seriously. "You understand you are to stay here? To stay right here with the Rangers?"

Pancho barked again and pranced around Little Jim.

"I see that leg does not hurt you so much now. You are very frisky."

Pancho had almost forgotten the wound in his leg. Now he limped slightly to show that his leg was not yet entirely well. He knew expressions of sympathy would come. He liked that.

"Your leg does hurt, after all," said Little Jim tenderly.

Pancho whined his appreciation.

"Come, we must go!"

Pancho danced happily again and ran ahead of Little Jim as they walked back toward the pueblo plaza. Little Jim squared his shoulders as he walked toward the ambulance which was already hitched to the horses. Bill was sitting in the driver's seat.

"Don Francisco will stay," he said to Bill.

"That's good," laughed Bill. "Jump up here now. We must be on our way."

Little Jim placed one moccasined foot on the hub of the front wheel and caught the rim in his hands. Pulling himself up into the ambulance, he sat beside Bill Wiswald. He looked straight ahead, his chin in the air.

No one said a word. The Rangers glanced at Pancho and then at Little Jim. Pancho stood, his tail wagging, his ears pricked forward, his mouth open in a grin. The wagon moved off. Pancho did not move. Little Jim did not look back.

Finally the group of Rangers broke up, and each started off to his duty. Pancho remained in the spot where Little Jim had left him. As the wagon moved away he sank on his haunches and gave a soft whimper.

When the horseman and ambulance were out of sight, Pancho turned and walked across the square to Jim Gault's quarters. He sniffed the doorstep, turned around several times, then lay down and curled up. His head sank on his front paws. He gave a long sigh.

Then Pancho remembered something. He remembered the bone he had buried several weeks before beneath the tree near the river. In a business-like way he got up and trotted off, his tail curled and a big grin on his face.

ABOUT THE AUTHOR

BRUCE GRANT, author, war correspondent, and free-lance writer, was born in 1893 in Wichita Falls, Texas. Educated at private schools, he attended the University of Kentucky. He left college for newspaper work, first in Louisville, Kentucky, and later in Chicago and New York. During World War I Grant served as a lieutenant with the 60th Field Artillery; in World War II he was sent to Europe as a war correspondent and chief of the London foreign news bureau of his paper.

A member of naval and historical organizations, a traveler, and a craftsman, he has based much of his writing on these interests and experiences. He is the author of many books, including *Warpath, Six Gun, Longhorn,* and *Leopard Horse Canyon.* He lives with his wife in Evanston, Illinois.